A Brush with Death

ALSO BY ELIZABETH J. DUNCAN

The Cold Light of Mourning

A Brush with Death

A PENNY BRANNIGAN MYSTERY

Elizabeth J. Duncan

Minotaur Books

A Thomas Dunne Book

New York

This is a work of fiction. All of the characters, organizations, and events portrayed in this novel are either products of the author's imagination or are used fictitiously.

A THOMAS DUNNE BOOK FOR MINOTAUR BOOKS.
An imprint of St. Martin's Publishing Group.

A BRUSH WITH DEATH. Copyright © 2010 by Elizabeth J. Duncan.
All rights reserved. Printed in the United States of America. For information,
address St. Martin's Press, 175 Fifth Avenue, New York, N.Y. 10010.

www.thomasdunnebooks.com
www.minotaurbooks.com

Library of Congress Cataloging-in-Publication Data

Duncan, Elizabeth J.
    A brush with death : a Penny Brannigan mystery / Elizabeth
J. Duncan.—1st ed.
        p. cm.
    "A Thomas Dunne book."
    ISBN 978-0-312-62282-4
    1. Women artists—Fiction.   2. Murder—Investigation—Fiction.
    3. City and town life—Wales—Fiction.   4. Wales—Fiction.   I. Title.
    PR9199.4.D863B78 2010
    813'.6—dc22

2010008716

First Edition: July 2010

10 9 8 7 6 5 4 3 2 1

In Loving Memory
Irene Theresa Lynch Campbell

Acknowledgments

Thank you to everyone who wrote to me after the publication of *The Cold Light of Mourning* with kind words of praise and encouragement. I am so grateful for your support, and hope this book lives up to your expectations.

A special shout-out to the wonderful librarians who embraced my first book. I love the idea that readers in, say, La Grange, Illinois, or Llanrwst, North Wales, can check this book out of their local library and, I hope, enjoy it.

Heartfelt thanks to the library ladies in Conwy, North Wales, who organized an evening for me and got everything absolutely right: Gaynor L. Jones, Cheryl Hesketh, Rhian Williams, Myfanwy Evans Jones, and Rhian Owen. (Beautiful Welsh names!)

Thank you, Madeleine Matte and Carol Putt, for reading the first draft and suggesting huge improvements.

And speaking of improvements, I am grateful to the editorial team at St. Martin's Press, notably the legendary Ruth Cavin and the patient, forgiving Toni Plummer. Also in New York, thank you to my agent, Dominick Abel, for wise counsel, direction, and guidance.

Thank you, Dr. Pete Wedderburn, for your veterinary counsel in the examination of Robbie, the Cairn terrier.

To Diane Mosher and Lea Milbury, thank you for the fun and friendship that inspired a loving relationship in this novel. Brian Sherwin in Llanrwst, I appreciate your daily tweets, although they make me long for the valley, and thank you for suggesting the sketching and walking route.

Special thanks to Dennis and Sybil Walker, who so kindly give Dolly wonderful vacations in their Hamilton, Ontario, garden while I am walking those beautiful Welsh hills and calling it research.

And finally, to my son, Lucas Walker, who was with me on the very first visit to Llanrwst and who brings joy and meaning to my life, wherever we are.

A Brush with Death

One

$\mathcal{P}$enny Brannigan awoke disoriented and confused. What on earth was she doing in the old-fashioned spare bedroom of Emma Teasdale's cottage? Why wasn't she at home in her own bed in the small, tidy flat above her manicure salon?

And then, through the just-woke-up muzziness, it all came back to her. She had recently inherited Jonquil Cottage, today was Sunday, and she had just spent her first night in her new home.

She kicked back the rumpled duvet, sat up, and looked about. The subdued light of a cheerless, rainy late-summer morning revealed an outdated pattern of orange poppies on yellowed wallpaper that had started to peel away from the ceiling and a substantial layer of dust on shabby, mismatched furniture. The room gave off a musty feel of neglect and the air was so close and stale that she leaned over to turn the latch of the small, leaded window beside the bed and pushed it open. When the first breath of cool, damp air from the garden filled her lungs, she felt her spirits lift as a feeling of excitement and anticipation began to creep in. She hopped out of bed, found her slippers, and padded across the hall to the loo.

A few minutes later she was standing at the bottom of the stairs. In front of her was the door that led to the street; to her right, the sitting room and dining area; and adjacent to that, toward the back of the cottage, a small kitchen which gave access to a partially walled garden, now somewhat overgrown but well laid out with mature pear trees espaliered along the south-facing brick wall.

With her hand resting on the banister, she surveyed the sitting room. What little light managed to filter through the closed curtains on this grey morning bathed the room in a soft, desolate luminosity, giving it the abandoned look of a place someone had once loved but would never be coming home to.

Although Penny had realized that the charming Welsh cottage would require major renovations to shift it out of the 1960s, she had decided to live in it before undertaking any drastic changes so she could get a feel for it, get to know it, and discover what she liked and what she didn't. She wanted to modernize it but in a way that would respect its history and the memory of its previous owner.

But there are too many memories crowded in here, she thought, memories that are not mine. Other people, from other times, living other lives.

Penny, a Canadian in her fifties, had met Emma when she arrived in the Welsh market town of Llanelen, decades ago.

Over the years, their friendship had grown, and Penny had been deeply saddened when Emma passed away. To Penny's astonishment, the retired schoolteacher who had never married and had no close relatives, had bequeathed the cottage and its contents to her, along with a substantial amount of money.

Although Penny had visited the cottage many times, it was different now. When you're a guest in someone's home, you don't see the precious, secret things that have been carefully preserved and hidden away, to be held, savored, and reflected upon in quiet, private moments.

Emma, who had been ill for some time, had made a will and funeral plans but had not got round to dealing with her personal effects. Perhaps she thought she had more time to wrap up her affairs, Penny thought. And don't we all?

Today, she would have to start clearing out Emma's things, but first things first. Facing the centre of the sitting room window, she reached above her head and grabbed a curtain in each hand. With a smooth, sweeping motion, like tearing off a bandage, she ripped them apart and as they swooshed along their rail, a soft, moist light filled the room.

That's a bit better, she thought. And now, she must find the kettle.

Her friends Victoria Hopkirk and Detective Inspector Gareth Davies had dropped her off at the cottage yesterday, and she was well provisioned with the basics. A few minutes later, carrying a steaming cup of freshly brewed coffee and a bowl of cereal on a tray, she made her way back to the sitting room and sat down on the faded, sagging sofa.

Opening a new notebook, she crossed her legs, looked around, and began to make a list:

Internet (and computer)
LR—New curtains
New furniture
Paint—pale green/white trim?
No wallpaper!
Carpet?

She crossed that out and then wrote underneath it.

Hardwood floors

With pen poised above the page, she gazed critically about her, taking in the overflowing bookshelves that filled one wall, side tables, a small walnut writing desk, and a pair of matching wing chairs that had once been 1950s brown but had been recovered in a 1970s floral chintz. Then, setting the notebook down, she wandered over to the writing desk.

She picked up a small figurine of a stooping man clad in a brown robe and turned it over. Royal Doulton. Scrooge. She set it down, smiled, and inclined her head slightly. Emma had loved Christmas and had always been generous with her gifts. Scrooge, of all things!

She tugged on a drawer and heard a slightly metallic, rattling sound as something inside shifted. The drawer moved a couple of inches and then stuck. She pulled on it again, harder this time, and under protest, it slid all the way out. Sitting on top of a dog-eared *Reader's Digest,* beside a magnifying glass with a tortoiseshell handle, was a scratched and dented tin pencil box. Wondering if it was a gift from one of Emma's long-ago pupils, Penny picked it up and turned it over. The bottom was painted a distinctive green, and the cream-colored top featured a sketch of St. Paul's Cathedral with a pencil in the same shade of green as the base of the tin. The Harrods logo occupied pride of place on the top left corner of the lid.

Noting the box was missing a hinge, she pried it open. Inside, she found a tattered ten-shilling note, a National Westminster Bank plastic bag containing a commemorative coin marking the 1981 wedding of the Prince of Wales and Lady Diana Spencer, a key, a concert ticket stub, a square key fob featuring the octagonal red MG logo, and a black-and-white photo.

She set the box down, picked up the photo, moved closer to the window, and turned slightly so the light fell on the image she was holding.

Gazing back at her was what appeared to be a young Emma wearing black eyeliner and false eyelashes. She smiled shyly at the camera but with a secretive, subtle confidence, her eyes slightly closed against the sun. Her blond hair had been elaborately styled in a towering bouffant, with curls trailing down her cheeks and she was wearing a sleeveless mini dress with two rows of white buttons down the front. In her arms she cradled a black-and-white fox terrier puppy.

Penny's lips moved slightly as she noted the dark nail polish Emma was wearing and then turned the photo over. In Emma's precise, schoolteacher handwriting was written *Winnie, Menlove Avenue, Woolton, 1967.*

Penny replaced the photo in the tin, snapped the lid shut, and set the battered pencil box back in the drawer.

What am I to do with things like that, she wondered. This was going to be harder than she'd thought. Not only prying into every nook and cranny of Emma's life but also having to sort through her things and probably get rid of most of it.

She took a sip of lukewarm coffee, had a spoonful of soggy cereal, and then headed upstairs to get dressed.

At the top of the stairs she paused at the doorway to Emma's old bedroom. The day before, emotionally drained and physically exhausted, she had taken a long nap on Emma's bed, but now, in the cold light of morning, she knew she would never sleep in the bed in which Emma had died. Getting rid of it would be easy. As part of the cottage makeover, she had promised herself a fresh, serene new bedroom.

And that pleasant thought brought her to Gareth. She wondered what he was doing and decided to ring him to see if he could come over and give her a hand. The job might go better with two, and he'd be much more objective. None of Emma's stuff would mean anything to him, and in his line of work, he'd had plenty of practice going through other people's belongings in a detached, clinical way.

Just as she was about to duck into the spare room in search of her mobile phone, it rang. She smiled when she saw who it was.

"Oh, I was just thinking about you," she said, "and wondering if you'd give me a hand sorting out all this stuff."

A few moments later she laughed and ran down the stairs to answer the door.

He bent his head to enter the cottage and then, in one easy, wordless moment they wrapped their arms around each other. He held her for a few seconds as she rested her head against his chest. They stepped back and he smiled at her upturned face.

"Right, then," he said, turning around to retrieve a large

bouquet of red and white carnations and two bottles of white wine he'd set down on the front step. "These are for you."

Penny smiled as she accepted his gifts. "I'll find a vase for these and put the wine in the fridge," she said.

"The flowers are for us," he said, nodding at them. "Red and white flowers for you. Canada, see? And then the red flowers and green ferns for me. The colours of Wales!"

Penny grinned at him.

"Oh, very charming! Did you think that up yourself, or did you have a bit of help?"

Gareth gave her a sheepish grin.

"Well, Bethan did say I was not to arrive empty-handed, but I figured out the bit about the colours myself."

"Well, they are lovely and it was very sweet of you. And Bethan," she added.

Bethan Morgan was Gareth's energetic young sergeant; the three had come to know one another over the summer as Penny helped the two police officers investigate the case of a missing bride.

Gareth stepped into the sitting room and looked around. "Doesn't seem to me that you've got too far. What have you done?"

Penny winced and waved a hand in a vague flap of defeat.

"Ah, like that, is it?"

She nodded.

"You do surprise me. Your old flat was so uncluttered, and I would have thought it would be easy to get rid of someone else's things because you've got no attachment to them. Unless, of course, you just happen to like something. Anyway, I've brought a few boxes so we can make a start. We'll sort it all into piles—one for the charity shop, one for the rubbish, and one for the things you want to keep. I think we should pack up as much as we can so the decorating will be easier. Let's start with the walls. You're an artist, so dealing with the paintings shouldn't be too difficult."

"You're right," agreed Penny. "I know what I like and what can go." Besides her manicure business, Penny painted scenic watercolours featuring the beautiful landscapes around Llanelen. She loved rambling through the valley, with easel and paintbrushes, capturing the timeless beauty of the deep greens and purples of the ancient, majestic hills that cradled the town.

She pointed to the small watercolour that hung over the desk.

"See that one? It's the first painting I did when I came to Llanelen. I gave it to Emma to thank her for being so good to me when she gave me a bed for a night or two." She smiled at him and opened her arms in an expansive gesture that took in the whole room. "And now look what she gave me!"

He removed the painting carefully from its hook and set it on the small table in front of the window, where Penny and Emma had spent many hours solving jigsaw puzzles.

"Right. What's next?"

She pointed to a pair of Monet prints.

"Charity shop."

She walked across the room and took down a painting.

"But this one I've always liked, and I definitely want to keep it."

8

She turned it to show to him and then looked at it again.

"Funny, all the years I've seen it and liked it but never had a chance to really look at it up close. It's rather well done, in my opinion, although it does need a good cleaning."

The painting was oil on canvas and showed two people at a picnic, a red-and-white checkered cloth spread out on the grass between them. She could make out what looked like a still life on the tablecloth . . . glasses of wine, a bowl of fruit, a cheese plate, and half a loaf of bread on a cutting board, with a bread knife beside it. The people were facing each other, the woman in a flowered summer dress with her legs folded away to the side as she leaned on one hand. The man lay on his back with his feet toward the viewer, his hands tucked under his head. Behind them was a large bank of purple flowers.

"The perspective on this is really excellent, you see," said Penny, pointing at the male figure. "With him reclining like that it would have been too easy to have him look flat and out of proportion, but the artist has got it just right. I used to ask Emma about this painting, but she wouldn't tell me anything about it. Just turned away and changed the subject."

She squinted at the signature. "A. Jones."

Davies walked over to her, put his hand gently on her arm, and glanced at the painting.

"Well, I don't know anything about art, but if you like it, that's good enough," he said. "Now, what do you want to do about that one?" They turned their attention to a large water-colour of blowsy pink roses as Penny set the painting she held in her hand in the keep pile.

She wagged her head back and forth while she thought

about it. "I think I like it," she said finally. "Let's keep it for now. I can find a place for it. Maybe in the new guest room."

Then, as Emma had always loved music, they started in on her rather extensive record and CD collections.

"We'll get rid of the old vinyl records," Penny said. "I don't want them, and I don't want the old record player or hi-fi or whatever it's called. But I'll keep the CDs. They don't take up too much space. They're mostly classical, but as I recall there's some good old pop stuff in there. She loved the Beatles, Emma did."

They moved on to the bookcases and started sorting out the contents. Most went into the charity-shop pile, although Gareth kept a couple of thrillers for himself, and by late morning they had filled several boxes. Penny hesitated when they came to the row of Emma's notebooks and personal journals. Emma had kept extensive commentaries on the day-to-day details of her life, including observations on the personalities and characters of hundreds of her pupils over the years. Her assessment of one student in particular had helped in the investigation of the missing bride.

"What's the matter?" Davies asked.

"I don't know what to do about the journals," Penny replied. "It seems a shame to bin them, but there are so many and I doubt I'd ever need them again. I certainly don't want to read them."

She looked at him as if asking him to make the decision. Gareth pulled out a slim red volume marked *1982* on its spine and riffled through it.

"Do you think you'll want to know what she wore to a coffee morning at the church on October first or what she had for dinner a few days later?"

Penny shook her head, and together they pulled the little books off the shelves and boxed them up for the rubbish.

"Oh, look," he said a few minutes later, holding up a Scrabble game with two elastic bands wrapped around the box, holding the tattered lid in place. "I like a game of Scrabble every now and then. Do you? Might as well keep it. Could come in handy on a long winter night. As long as all the letters are there, of course. We could count them out later, maybe. Let's keep it for now, shall we?"

As Penny murmured her agreement, he set it down, then picked it up again at both ends and gently tipped it back and forth.

"Feels a bit heavy."

Penny glanced at it and then went on with her book sorting.

"I expect there's a dictionary in the box. Some people keep one with the game so they have it handy for the challenges. I haven't come across one on the shelves, and Emma must have had one, so I expect it's in there."

"Happens you're right."

Penny tucked her hand under her chin and pursed her lips.

"Odd, that game of Scrabble, though. We used to do jigsaws together, but she never brought that game out."

Davies grinned. "Maybe she thought you'd be too much of a challenge for her."

Penny gave a little snort.

"The other way round, more like."

Finally, Davies stepped back and assessed the boxes they had filled.

"That wasn't so bad now, was it? Why don't we drop the

charity boxes off at the shop, just to get them out of the way, and then I'll take you to lunch?"

Penny nodded.

"Just give me a few minutes to wash up and get changed. Won't be long." She touched him lightly on the arm as if to reassure herself, and then turned toward the stairs.

As she disappeared, Davies sat down on the sofa to wait. The place really did have lovely bones, and he had no doubt that when Penny was finished with it, the cottage would be beautiful. Light and airy, in soft, modern colours with all the right accent pieces and looking like the cover spread on an interior design magazine.

A few minutes later she was back, and they began shifting the boxes out the front door.

"You know," he said as Penny locked the door, "this business of clearing away old stuff gets better as you go along. At first you don't know what to keep, but once you start chucking things out, it gets easier to toss it than to keep it. At least, that's the way it was for me when my wife died."

Penny grimaced as she put her key in her handbag.

"Let's not go there today," she said. "Dealing with Emma's death is quite enough for one morning."

Two

They returned after lunch with a renewed sense of purpose and set about finishing the living room. If it's neither useful nor ornamental, it's got to go, Gareth had reminded her, and they were now making good progress. A lot of things had been removed, and Penny thought the place was looking better already. With the living room done, they started on the kitchen. Penny told him she was going to get a new kitchen put in but would keep the old slate floor.

"And you'll keep the Welsh dresser, of course," he replied.

"Of course!"

"Well, have we done enough for one day?" he asked a couple of hours later. "Should we open a bottle of wine, do you think? It's cleared up nicely, so we could sit in the garden. I'll make a few notes on what needs doing out there. We can tidy it up and get it ready for next spring. Plant some bulbs this fall, maybe."

A few minutes later, wineglasses in hand, they plopped down into a pair of old striped deck chairs they had found leaning up against the wall.

"Listen," said Gareth as he shifted in his chair. "I want to talk to you about something serious. Now that you're in the cottage, and a little off the beaten path, you need to be careful about locking up at night and when you go out. It's deserted here after dark, and with nobody about, anything can happen."

Penny nodded.

"I mean it. We've seen an awful increase lately in rural crime. Lead ripped off churches, break-ins, you name it. Even sheep stealing."

As Penny started to smile, he held up his hand and frowned.

"No, it's serious. Farmers come out in the morning and their sheep are gone." He shrugged. "It gets worse. Their dogs have usually been killed or badly injured. Really cruel, un-speakable acts. Mutilations. Awful."

As Penny gazed into her wineglass, he reached over and touched her shoulder.

"I didn't want to upset you, but do, please, be careful. There are some really nasty people about and I'd hate for you . . ."

His voice trailed off as her eyes widened.

"Well, you know what I mean. I wouldn't want any harm to come to you."

He struggled to his feet.

"God, these chairs are awful! Why on earth were they once so popular? You can't set them up, they're uncomfortable, and impossible to get out of! They should have all gone down with the *Titanic*—every last bloody one of them!"

Penny smiled as she held her glass up to him.

"I'm pretty sure the *Titanic* deck chairs were wooden. I saw one once at an exhibit in Halifax."

"Halifax? Oh, right, Nova Scotia."

A few moments later he handed her refilled wineglass back to her and then clattered about with his chair.

"Ooof," he said as he lowered himself gingerly into it. "Look, as my housewarming gift, please let me get you a decent pair of garden chairs. And these ones will do nicely to start the fire on bonfire night."

"Great," agreed Penny. "Thank you."

Gareth took a sip of his wine and grimaced. "Next time," he asked, "would it be all right if I brought along a few cans of beer? I like a glass of wine with a meal well enough, but there are times when a glass of beer just seems to hit the spot."

They leaned back in their chairs and examined their surroundings. Enclosed on two sides by a brick wall, the garden had become a wild tangle of neglect in the months before and after Emma's death. Although badly in need of weeding and grooming, the space had wonderful potential, and Gareth had assured Penny that with her help he could soon have the gardens, front and back, knocked back into shape.

"Would you like a vegetable patch next summer?" he asked. "It's become very trendy to grow your own. You can't beat fresh peas right out of the garden, garnished with a bit of mint. Mind you, you have to be careful with the mint or it'll take over every inch of ground you've got. But there are ways to keep it under control. And I expect you'll be wanting a barbecue."

15

They talked for a few moments about their plans for the week. Penny and Victoria had recently learned that an attractive but rundown stone building situated on the River Conwy was coming up for sale, and they wanted to look it over. They had formed a business partnership and now that Victoria had received her divorce settlement, they planned to expand the manicure salon into a larger, more inclusive spa operation offering lots of additional services.

Gareth and Penny sat quietly for a few more moments, enjoying the late-afternoon sunlight that illuminated everything it touched, pricking everything with a soft, intense pinkish hue. Then, with a small sigh, he struggled once again to his feet.

He reached down a hand to Penny and pulled her up and out of her chair.

"Time for me to go," he said. "Don't you hate that time on a Sunday afternoon when the weekend starts to feel over?"

As they made their way into the kitchen, he glanced at the Welsh dresser. Made of solid, seasoned oak, it was decorated with carved sides and featured two plate racks over a base of three drawers and two small cupboards on the bottom. Carefully arranged on the plate racks was Emma's favourite tea set in a feminine pattern called Sweet Violets. The pretty cups and saucers were dusty.

"Have you checked for a secret compartment in that dresser?" Gareth asked, pointing at it.

"No! I didn't know there'd be one. Never even thought of it."

"My grandmother had a dresser just like it. She was so proud of it. We used to go round to visit her on Sunday afternoon and stay for our tea, and my mum, bless her, would take away Granny's laundry and bring it back all washed and ironed the next week. She showed me how it worked when I was about ten. Let's have a look."

He walked over to the dresser, removed the bread and butter plates from the lower shelf, and set them carefully on the counter. Returning to the dresser, he tapped along the back of it and then slid his hand slowly along the underside of the shelf where the delicate dishes from the tea service had been moments before.

"Ah," he said softly, "hand me a knife, would you? One with a sharp point." Taking the paring knife Penny gave him, he released a hidden clasp, then gently pushed on the rear section of the cabinet. A small piece of board gave way, revealing a pigeonhole. He groped about inside and withdrew a small packet, which he handed to Penny.

"Here you go," he said, handing it over. "Probably the most valuable thing she owned."

It was a bundle of about two dozen letters, tied in a purple ribbon with small white dots.

"Well," said Gareth, "I'll leave you to it. I've got to get back to Llandudno, so I'll ring you tomorrow. You can tell me all about them then, if you like."

They walked together to the front door, where he lightly kissed her good-bye. She stood in the doorway and watched as he made his way to his car, turning to wave at her before setting off.

Still holding the packet of letters, she walked over to the sofa and sat down. Slowly, she untied the ribbon, withdrew the first letter from its envelope and gently unfolded it. It gave off a weak scent of lavender.

Liverpool, Sunday, April 15, 1967

My dear girl, she read. *I couldn't believe my great good luck when on a dull, boring Saturday afternoon, you appeared at my table in a crowded railway station buffet and asked if you might sit down.*

She stopped reading, turned the letter over, and looked at the signature.

Yours,

Al J.

Could Al J. be A. Jones? She got up and walked over to the painting showing the couple at the picnic, gazed at the signature for a moment, and then returned to the sofa. Thoughtfully, she refolded the letter, placed it back in its envelope, and then tied everything back up in the purple ribbon. Wondering where to put the letters, she settled on the desk, placed the packet in the drawer, and closed it. She started back toward the sofa, but then stopped, turned around, and retraced her steps. Opening the desk drawer, she withdrew the Harrods' pencil case, flipped it open, withdrew the photo, and looked at the back: *1967.*

"Nineteen sixty-seven," she said softly. "I wonder."

Holding the photo by the lower right corner, she tapped it against the palm of her left hand. I wonder, she thought, who took the photo. That's always the interesting bit. There's the person in the photo, and then there's the unseen presence of the photographer. There were at least two people there that day. And then there's the fox terrier, Winnie. Penny knew that Emma had liked dogs, but she had never mentioned this pretty little terrier with her adorable black-and-white face and a few freckles sprinkled across the bridge of her nose.

Yawning, Penny set the photo down on the desk and

glanced at her watch. It was early evening, much too early for bed, but she was tired and the wine was making her sleepy. I'll just lie down for an hour or so, she thought, then get up, have some soup or something light to eat, and then perhaps make a start on sorting out that spare bedroom. As dusk began to settle over the room, she reached for the banister and slowly climbed the stairs.

Three hours later, she awoke in darkness and groaned. Although the room was shrouded in the velvet blackness of night, she felt that morning was still a long way off. Cold and stiff, she stretched out to switch on the bedside lamp, looked at the clock. Oh God, she thought. Eleven. There goes my night's sleep. Sighing, she touched the button on her clock radio and lay there in the dark, embraced by the intimacy of the unmistakable, sweet voice of John Fogerty.

Clouds of mystery pouring
Confusion on the ground

It's no good, she thought, realizing she was famished. I might as well go downstairs and see what there is to eat.

A few minutes later, a glass of water in one hand and a cheese and onion sandwich in the other, she plunked herself down on the sofa and switched on the television. She slumped back and idly changed channels until she found herself watching a news item about a shopkeeper who had been fined for putting out his rubbish in the wrong-coloured bin bag.

"What next?" she asked the screen, and then suddenly sat up straight.

Moments later she slipped out the back door and headed for

the pile of boxes she and Gareth had set out earlier for the rubbish. She opened one and, not seeing what she was looking for, closed it up and moved on to the next box. In the fourth one she found Emma's old notebooks and journals and, grabbing the box by the cardboard flap, dragged it inside. She left it on the kitchen floor, glanced at the dresser, and then reached back to lock the door.

On Monday afternoon she had arranged to meet Victoria outside the office of Jenkins and Jones to finalize the legal details of their business partnership. When Victoria was ten minutes late, Penny wasn't sure whether she should be annoyed or worried. And then she saw her hurrying around the corner, her dress billowing slightly in the breeze.

"I am so sorry!" Victoria wailed. "I got held up with a phone call just as I was leaving. Bronwyn called and it seemed rude to cut her off. She wanted to know if, oh, never mind, it can wait. We'd better get in there."

Victoria was now living in Penny's old flat above the manicure salon. She had arrived in Llanelen for what had been meant to be a bit of rest and relaxation several months ago but, for many reasons, had decided to stay on. She and Penny had found they had much in common, and as their friendship deepened, they had started working together.

The smell of fresh paint greeted them as they entered the office of Richard Jones, the senior partner.

A small, tidy, bald man in his sixties, who favoured a three-piece suit, he had looked after many of the townsfolk's legal affairs for decades. It was he who had handled the execution of Emma's will, including turning over the cottage to Penny.

The receptionist greeted them politely but coolly, sending a mildly reproving message for their lateness. They were the last appointment of the day, and it was obvious from her manner that she had better things to do than hang about waiting for them.

"He's been expecting you," she said primly, nodding in the direction of a closed door. "You're to go right in."

Richard Jones stood up to greet them as they entered his office. Here, too, was the smell of fresh paint; the windows overlooking the street had been washed and the refurbishment gave everything a look of understated, refreshed professionalism.

If the receptionist had been upset because they were late, Jones showed no signs of concern.

"Good afternoon, ladies," he said, gesturing to the two chairs facing his desk. "Please, take a seat. So very nice to see you. Yes, indeed. Now then, shall we get down to business?"

He reached for a file and began explaining the terms of their agreement, who would contribute what, how the partnership could be dissolved, the importance of each one having a will.

But Penny was not listening.

On the wall behind Jones was a painting that seemed to be the companion of the one she had in her own sitting room. It depicted the same picnic in the same spot but a different couple.

In her painting, the couple was sitting at the left and right of the painting. In this version, another couple was sitting at

21

the top and bottom. If you were to blend the two images, she realized, you would have four people at the same picnic, one person on each side of the checkered tablecloth and the bank of purple flowers behind them. Unlike Emma's painting, however, this one looked as if it had recently been cleaned and its colours were bright and true.

"And all this notwithstanding," Jones was saying, "all property that you might purchase will be held jointly; so in effect, you will be equal partners not only in the running of the business but in the legal holdings. You will each be entitled to fifty percent of the profits and you will each be responsible for fifty percent of the risk."

He looked from one to the other.

"I think this agreement reflects your wishes. Do you have any questions?

"Sorry," said Penny. "But yes, I have a question. Who painted that painting behind you? It was A. Jones, wasn't it? Was he a relative of yours?"

If he was surprised by her off-topic question, Jones did not show it.

"Yes, as a matter of fact, to both your questions," he said, shifting in his seat to glance over his shoulder at it. "We recently rediscovered this painting hidden away in our parents' home and after the decorating, we decided to hang it. Rather nice for what it is, don't you think?"

Penny nodded as she stood up.

"It is indeed," she said. "I wonder if I might take a closer look at it." Catching Victoria's dark look, she apologized and sat down again.

"If you're ready, then, let's just get the signing out of the way," Jones suggested, "and then you may look at the painting for as long as you wish."

With Jones occasionally pointing to a red dot on the papers, accompanied by a soft "and now again just here, please," Victoria and Penny signed the papers.

"Congratulations, ladies," Jones said at the end of the signing. "You are now official co-owners of the Llanelen Spa. I understand the next step is the purchase of property, and I hope I may be of service to you in all aspects of your venture."

He beamed from one to the other and clasped his hands together.

"Now, Penny, you were interested in this painting."

"Yes," said Penny. "You see there's one like it in Emma's, well, my sitting room, and I wanted to know more about it. Do you know anything about the artist? Was he a good friend of Emma's?"

"Well, I can certainly tell you about the artist," said Jones. "But the thing is, A. Jones was a she. She was my sister, Alys Jones."

"Alys! Why did Emma never mention her to me?" Penny asked. "What happened to her? Is she still alive? May I go to see her?"

"Sadly, no," Jones replied. "She died in 1970."

Penny and Victoria glanced at each other as he began to gather up the documents they had just signed.

"How did she die, if you don't mind me asking?"

"It was a hit-and-run accident, Penny. They never did find out who did it."

He sighed. "It was so long ago. Not much can be done about it now, eh? She was quite a well-respected artist in her day, I think, but you'd know more about that than I would."

After a moment, he placed his pen in the holder on his desk, locked his desk drawer, dropped the key into his vest pocket, and smiled at them.

"Well, ladies, I think that's everything, so I needn't keep you any longer. All the best on your new venture."

Three

I've got some nice white wine in the fridge. Why don't you come round and we'll drink to our new partnership," Penny said. "Of course, we'll do something bigger and better later—make it more official. We'll have a proper launch party when we open the spa."

Victoria agreed and they set off on the walk through the town to Jonquil Cottage.

"Something's bothering you, Penny," Victoria remarked, "and I think it's to do with that painting. It seems to have really spooked you. What's the matter? Is it about that artist's death? Who was she, anyway?"

Penny shook her head.

"I'll show you when we get there," she replied, "and tell

you all about it. Or at least what I know so far. What was it you were saying about Bronwyn earlier?"

"Oh, that. Right, she wants to know if we'll help out with the church jumble sale. Sort things out, put prices on them, that kind of thing. It's not for a while yet, but I told her I would and said I'd ask you. I think she's also hoping that you'll donate any of Emma's things that you don't want."

"Damn!" said Penny. "I should have remembered her sale is coming up. We dropped off tons of stuff yesterday at the charity shop. I'll have to see what else there is. I haven't done the bedrooms yet, so I'm sure there'll be loads of clothes there for her. Good stuff, too. Not that old lady polyester rubbish."

She smiled.

"Good thing you reminded me. Bronwyn would have been very cross with me."

As the wife of Rector Thomas Evans, Bronwyn was involved in many aspects of town life and carried out the traditional demands of her role with great enthusiasm and empathy.

As she made a mental note to keep the church sale in mind, Penny and her friend turned down the small street that led to the cottage, and a few minutes later Victoria was gazing around the sitting room.

"I can see you've made great progress here. Everything looks decluttered, and a new coat of paint will go a long way to freshening everything up. What are you going to do about the floor? I'd go with hardwood, if I were you. Maybe get some of that new bamboo. Very ecological."

Penny nodded, headed for the fridge, and then handed Victoria a glass of white wine.

"Here," she said, leading Victoria to the table where the

paintings that had been removed from the walls the day before were stacked. "What do you make of this?"

She pointed to the A. Jones painting.

Victoria bent over to take a closer look.

"I see what you mean, but I don't get it. Would someone do two paintings of the same scene? Why not put everyone in the same painting if they were all there at the same time? I wonder, though. Two couples at a picnic? Wouldn't it be more usual for a couple to go on a picnic by themselves? Just two people enjoying a bit of privacy, outdoors, over a simple meal?" She gazed at the painting. "Do you think it could be two views of the same couple? And who are they?"

"I don't know yet, but I do want a closer look at Richard Jones's painting. Do you think he'd let me borrow it? Or at least photograph it?"

Victoria thought for a moment.

"You know, he might, if you showed him this one and explained it all to him. He knows you're an artist and he'd understand why you're interested. But I think you should bring him, um, that one," she said, pointing at the painting of the pink roses. "You can't leave him with an empty picture hook behind his desk. He'd be more likely to lend you his painting if you offered to fill up the space with something."

"You're right," said Penny. "I'll do that. But here, there's something else."

She removed the packet of letters from the drawer in the side table and showed them to Victoria.

"I think these letters are from that artist, A. Jones. They're to Emma. I haven't read them properly. Gareth found them yesterday in the Welsh dresser, and I wasn't in the right frame of mind to read them. I glanced at one of them, but it seemed invasive to read it. Didn't feel comfortable. I guess they drum it into us when we're young that we just don't read other people's mail."

After a moment she sat on the sofa, folded her arms, and then continued. "I wasn't even sure if I should read them. I mean, really, what would be the point?"

She paused for a moment.

"And, you know, Emma was such a private person, I think she'd be horrified to think that someone was reading her letters. Maybe I should just destroy them."

"Or," said Victoria, punctuating her sentence with a little nod, "maybe she left them there for you to find because she wanted you to read them."

A thoughtful silence descended between them.

"Well, what about this, then," said Victoria a few moments later. "I'll make dinner and you can have a good old think about what you want to do about the letters."

"I like the dinner part, but I'll leave the letters. To be honest, I think I should be alone when I read them. That is, if I read them." Penny took a sip of wine and settled further into the sofa, the letters resting on her lap.

Victoria nodded, made her way to the kitchen, and clattered about in the cupboards looking for a large pot.

"Mmm, this is really good," said Penny about half an hour later, turning over a forkful of pasta tossed with butter and freshly grated parmesan cheese. "You're a genius at making something from nothing."

Victoria smiled her thanks.

"You know, there's something I've been wondering about . . ." She fell silent.

28

"Yes?" prompted Victoria. "What? What have you been wondering about?"

"Well, what kind of person would kill someone in a hit-and-run? How could you drive away, leaving someone injured and lying in the street? How could you not stop and try to help?"

"A selfish, frightened person?" suggested Victoria.

"Or what if the person was drunk and afraid of the police?" Penny mused. "How would that person feel when he woke up the next morning with a bad hangover and realized he'd killed someone? Or, even worse, what if the person wasn't dead, and died later, but might have been saved if the driver had stopped to help?"

"I think it would depend on the person," Victoria replied. "I reckon some folks would get themselves down to the nearest police station right away and others would live out the rest of their days as if nothing had happened. And maybe others would be somewhere in between."

Penny nodded slowly.

"There's something else. Richard Jones didn't seem all that upset. If your sister had been killed, wouldn't you show a bit more emotion?"

"Penny," said Victoria gently, "this is news to you, but for him it happened a long time ago. She died more than thirty years ago. He got on with his life. He moved on because he had to. He's learned to live with it."

Penny nodded.

"And anyway," Victoria added, "we don't know how he reacted at the time. He might have been really cut up. But remember, too, he's of that generation. They don't show much emotion. They just accept things the way they are and get on with it."

"I guess you're right," Penny agreed. "But I want to find out everything I can about this artist Alys Jones. She and Emma must have meant something to each other or they wouldn't have corresponded. I'm starting to get very curious about that accident, and I'd like to find out what happened to her." She shrugged. "So I guess that's the point of reading the letters. It's a place to start, and maybe the letters will shed a bit of light on what happened."

She wiped her lips on her napkin and set it down beside her plate.

"I wish I had the Internet so I could look something up."

"Well, that's not a problem," said Victoria. "You can stop into the library in the morning and use the computer there."

"I know I can," said Penny with a touch of impatience and petulance, "but I want the Internet here so I can look things up whenever I want. Like right now."

"Well, if it's really bothering you, maybe I can help. I'll call Bronwyn's cousin—you know where I stayed that time and where the kids are. Teenagers can't go five minutes without the Internet. What do you want to know?"

"I want to know where a street is. Here, I'll write it down for you."

Victoria placed the call on her mobile and spoke for a few moments. She gestured to Penny to hand her a pen, scribbled a few notes, and then rang off.

"He Googled it and the street came up right away. It's in Liverpool. And you'll never guess who lived at number two fifty-one Menlove Avenue."

She nodded at Penny.

"Go on, guess!"

After a few moments, she added, "Think about it! Liverpool. It was one of *them*."

Penny's eyes widened.

"John Lennon. He lived at number two fifty-one Menlove Avenue with his aunt Mimi. But by 1967, of course, he was long gone and the Beatles were almost over."

Penny pushed her plate away and folded her hands on the table.

"Right. Let's see what we've got, then. Emma knew an artist or was friends with an artist, who was killed in a hit-and-run. She has a painting by that artist hanging on her wall, and our solicitor, who was the brother of that artist, has a companion painting hanging on his wall. His painting has been in storage and out of sight for years. And then there's a photo of Emma taken in 1967 in John Lennon's garden with a fox terrier named Winnie."

Victoria smiled.

"Well, we don't know for sure that it was John Lennon's garden, but it could be the same street. Still, that's about what it looks like."

She picked up a few plates from the table, carried them into the kitchen, and set them down on the counter.

"Would you like tea?" she called over her shoulder. "I'm putting the kettle on."

When there was no answer, she turned around and looked at the table. She was talking to thin air; the table was empty.

From the living room the sound of John Lennon singing "In My Life" filled the small, cozy rooms. As the kettle started to boil in the kitchen behind her, Victoria walked quietly past the table to the sitting room entrance and peered in. She watched as Penny tucked a wayward strand of red hair behind her left ear and then removed a purple ribbon with white polka dots from a small bundle of letters and set the ribbon on the sofa beside her. Taking up the first envelope, Penny set the rest down on the coffee table. She held the letter in her hand, poised to unfold it.

She looked up at Victoria, smiled weakly, and bent her head over the letter.

"Sorry, couldn't wait."

A few moments later Victoria set a cup of tea down on the small table near Penny's elbow and gently touched her shoulder.

"I'll see myself out," she said softly. "Call me tomorrow."

"Mmm. Thanks," Penny said without looking up but giving her a vague wave of acknowledgment.

Then, as the front door quietly closed, she started again to read the first letter.

Liverpool, Sunday, April 15, 1967
My dear girl, I couldn't believe my great good luck when on a dull, boring Saturday afternoon, you appeared at my table in a crowded railway station buffet and asked if you might sit down.

Four

LIVERPOOL, SATURDAY, APRIL 14, 1967

Emma Teasdale glanced at her watch as she left the Royal Philharmonic Hall and headed off along Hope Street on her way to Lime Street station. From years of enjoying Saturday afternoon concerts at the Phil she knew how to time it just right to have a cup of tea at the railway station buffet and then make the train and bus connections that would see her back home in Llanelen by about 8 P.M.

The sky had turned dark while she had been listening to Benjamin Britten's *War Requiem* and now a hard, driving rain was drenching the grey city. By the time she reached Mount Pleasant Street her feet were soaked through and the uplifted mood in which she had left the concert hall was deteriorating into deflated grumpiness.

Finally, by now in a resentful funk, she entered the station concourse, shook the rain off her umbrella, folded it up, and tucked it under her arm. Not surprisingly, at four o'clock on a rainy afternoon, the station buffet was crowded and the room was filled with a fragrant, steamy warmth. She ordered and paid for tea and a Welsh cake at the counter and, holding her tray, turned around looking for a place to sit. She had hoped to have a table to herself, as she was not in the mood for polite small talk with a stranger, but there was no empty table to be had. Spotting a table for two at the side of the room with a woman occupying one of the chairs, she headed for it.

"Excuse me," asked Emma, "would you mind terribly if I sat down?"

The woman looked up at her and smiled.

"No, no one's sitting there. Please join me." She closed what looked like a catalogue and helpfully pulled the vacant chair away from the table. Emma placed her cup and plate on the table, set the tray and umbrella beside her chair, sat down, and took a grateful sip of tea. She stole a glance at the woman, who had gone back to perusing the catalogue. She seemed about the same age as Emma, with short dark hair brushed back from her face and strong, well-defined features. Perhaps sensing Emma's gaze, the woman looked up from her reading and picked up the glass of brandy she had been nursing.

"So," she asked, peering coolly at Emma over the rim of her snifter, "what brings you to town on this dreary afternoon?"

"I've just been to a concert at the Phil," Emma replied. "I've a subscription and come every month or so."

A light silence hung between them in that defining instant when two strangers, for whatever reasons, decide in the first

34

few words they exchange whether they wish to get to know the other person better.

"And you?"

"Just been to an exhibit at the Walker Gallery over the road," she replied. And then after a moment, her face softened as her eyes explored Emma's face, and she smiled. "My name's Alys."

"I'm Emma. Nice to meet you."

"And where are you headed for now, Emma?"

"I live in Llanelen, but you've probably not even heard of it. Just a little town not too far from Llandudno."

Alys laughed.

"Oh, I've heard of it," she said, crossing her legs and leaning back in her chair. "This might be one of those small-world moments. I have family in Llanelen. My older brothers live and work there. Jones is my name."

"I probably teach their children, then, in the primary school!"

The two continued to chat, easily and eagerly, until Emma realized, with reluctance, that it was time to leave to catch the train to Chester where she would change for Llandudno. She pushed back her chair and reached for her gloves.

"I must be going," she said. "It was nice meeting you."

"And you," Alys replied. "I'll be on my way as well."

An intense attraction charged with longing crackled between them.

"You know," said Alys, maintaining eye contact while she reached for the umbrella Emma had placed between the chairs and offered it to its owner, "*The Sound of Music* is playing at the Odeon and I wondered if you might like to see it with me next week. We could go to an early showing and perhaps have a meal afterward."

"That sounds wonderful." Emma smiled, hoping the relief in her voice wasn't too obvious. "I'd like that very much." As she took the umbrella, their hands touched and they looked at each other with complete understanding.

"Well, that's settled then," said Alys. "Give me your address and I'll write you. Are you on the phone? I could ring you later in the week and we'll sort things out. Shall I walk you to your platform?"

The things I must do, Alys thought cheerfully a few minutes later, as she made her way to the station exit. Two hours of Julie Andrews and the kids singing those bloody awful songs. Whiskers on kittens! And then, unable to stop herself, she started to hum.

And so it began. They met the following week, and this time Emma was not traveling on a same-day return ticket. Their relationship deepened in the anonymity of Liverpool, a culturally sophisticated city where they conducted their affair in the loving privacy of Alys's small, north-facing flat in a red-brick Georgian house on Rodney Street, near the Liverpool School of Art, where she taught painting and drawing. Occasionally, Alys drove to Llanelen, but Emma was afraid to be seen with her in the small town, knowing that if their relationship became common knowledge, it would undoubtedly mean a scandalous end to the teaching job she loved so much and the livelihood it provided.

Three years flew by as they settled easily into a comfortable routine, sharing picnics under sunny skies, taking long drives in Alys's MG convertible, and living together as a couple in quiet domesticity. They wrote to each other when circumstances prevented their getting together—letters that Emma tied in a purple ribbon and hid in the Welsh dresser.

But early one morning in December 1970 their relationship came to an unexpected, violent end.

"Well, try to be here on time for the start of *Dad's Army*," said Emma over the telephone. "You know I like to see the programme from the beginning."

"I will," promised Alys.

Emma puttered about the cottage that evening, doing a little dusting and straightening up shelves that didn't really need tidying. She was always on edge when Alys visited. Although her cottage was fairly isolated, with only a few neighbours to worry about, and the wooded lot and fields behind it, she always felt they were being watched and that everyone must know about them.

That evening, a few moments before the familiar theme song began, Emma heard the back door open and seconds after that, wearing her green tweed coat, Alys was bounding into the room. *"Who do you think you are kidding, Mr. Hitler, if you think we're on the run?"* she sang as she took Emma in her arms and kissed her.

Laughing, the two flopped down on the sofa.

"Our meal's in the oven keeping warm until the programme's over," Emma said. "Here's some cheese and biscuits to tide you over, you stupid boy!"

Laughing at the popular catchphrase from the programme that everyone in Britain was using, Alys took the plate Emma handed to her and bit hungrily into a piece of cheddar. "Oh, and a bunch of grapes, too! Lucky old me!"

"Take your coat off," Emma commanded, "and I'll hang it up for you."

When the programme finished, Emma took their dinner from the oven and they sat together at the table. Emma glanced around to reassure herself that all the curtains were closed, while Alys poured them each a glass of wine.

"Relax," she said. "Stop fussing; there's nothing to worry about. Why are you so twitchy?"

"You know what the gossip machine is like around here," Emma replied, "and if certain people knew you were stopping here, it'd be in overdrive. I daren't even post my letters to you from the town post office—the post mistress is that nosey. I have to walk halfway to the next town and use the rural box outside the pub."

Emma took a sip of wine, put her glass down, and looked at her companion.

"Look, it's probably nothing, but I've had a feeling lately that I'm being watched. I noticed someone lounging about when I came out of the butcher's, and then I saw the same man again a few days later near the school. I have no idea who he is—never seen him before."

Alys pushed a bit of lamb chop around on her plate.

"Well, maybe he was a parent."

"No," said Emma. "I know all the parents and he's not one of them."

"What did he look like?"

"Rather tall, on the skinny side, and well, he looked a bit like a ferret. Had squinty eyes and a really mean look about him."

"Doesn't sound like anyone I know," said Alys. "This lamb is delicious. How did you make it?"

"I fried it," said Emma flatly, "same as I always do. Don't try to change the subject."

"Sorry, love," said Alys. "But I think you're worrying for nothing, just like you always do." Seeing Emma's downcast face, she reached for her. "I love your hands," she said softly, kissing Emma's fingers.

After dinner they tidied away the dishes and then cleared the table for a friendly game of Scrabble.

While Alys set up the board and turned the tiles facedown, Emma flipped through her collection of LPs.

Holding a black vinyl disc in her hand, she called through to Alys in the dining room. "How about Donovan? Are you in the mood for him?"

Alys nodded, poured herself a small glass of brandy, and as the opening guitar chords of "Catch the Wind" filled the two small rooms, the women selected their tiles and the match began.

About twenty minutes later Alys lit a small cigar, and smiled to herself as a look of triumph spread across Emma's face.

"Watch this," said Emma, as she laid down her tiles.

Q-U-E-E-N-L-Y

"And on a triple, too!" she exclaimed. "Let me add this up. Ten, eleven, twelve, thirteen . . ."

Alys laughed and then, sitting back in her chair, crossed her legs and stuck out her tongue a little, and with her thumb and middle finger removed a small piece of tobacco from the end of her tongue.

Emma stopped counting and glanced at her.

"That is so sexy," she said.

"What is?" asked Alys.

"When you do that thing with your tongue and your fingers."

Alys inclined her head slightly and tapped off the ash from her cigar.

"Only you would think something like that."

"Damn! Now you've made me lose my place and I'll have to start counting all over again. You're just getting cross because I'm going to win."

"No, I'm getting cross because you haven't asked me how the work on the new exhibition's coming along."

"Oh, I'm so sorry. I didn't think. How is it coming along?"

"Really well. It will be ready for the show in February. The curator is coming next week to look at the pieces to decide the order. I think we already know which ones will be included. But I haven't shown any of the work to anyone yet. Keeping it under wraps."

She looked anxiously at Emma.

"Of course you'll come to the opening, won't you?"

"Just try and keep me away."

They finished the game, declared Emma the winner, and then watched the television news. With a small sigh, Emma got up from the sofa, switched off the television, and went through the kitchen to make sure the back door was locked for the night. Alys checked the front door, and together they made their way upstairs to Emma's bedroom.

Alys removed a small box from the pocket of her trousers before hanging them over the back of a chair. She set the box on the bedside table, and when she and Emma were comfortably settled in bed, she put her arm around Emma, pulled her to her, and reached out to pick up the box.

"Look," she whispered, handing it to Emma. "I've got a little gift for you. I hope you like it."

She handed over the box and watched expectantly as Emma opened it. A slow smile spread across her face and she turned to Alys.

"Do you like it? Do you?" asked Alys eagerly. "I know it's not much, but it means something to us."

Nestled inside the box was a glass paperweight in which small purple flowers hung suspended.

"It's beautiful!" exclaimed Emma. "Oh, thank you so much."

"I'm glad you like it," whispered Alys. "I hope it will always remind you of how much I love you."

Emma set the globe on her bedside table. "I'll treasure it."

She switched off the bedside lamp, and the two slid down into the bed and wrapped their arms around each other.

"Alys?'

"Hm hmm."

"Do you think the day will ever come when we'll be able to live together openly? When we can really be who we are?"

"I don't know," mumbled Alys. "I hope so. At least that

way I'd be allowed to sleep here until it was light and maybe I'd even get some breakfast. I hate having to leave while it's dark just so no one will see me. All this creeping about—we haven't done anything wrong."

"Sorry, my darling, but you know how I feel about that. It makes me very nervous, you being here, but I wish you could stay forever."

Alys turned over and was soon sound asleep. Emma listened to her soft, gentle breathing and then snuggled up behind her.

Shortly before dawn, Alys stirred and came awake. She put her arms around her sleeping companion and kissed her. She held her for a few minutes and then whispered to her.

"Tell me I have to get up."

"You have to get up," replied Emma sleepily.

Alys groaned and slid out of bed. She dressed quickly in the cold bedroom and then reached for Emma, wrapped in warmth.

"Bye, then, love," she said. "See you soon. You will come to Liverpool for the weekend, won't you?"

Emma murmured and retreated into sleep. Alys tiptoed out of the bedroom and down the stairs. When she reached the bottom, she pulled a coat off the hooks in the small entranceway, made her way through the dark, silent sitting and dining rooms to the back door. Patting her trouser pocket to make sure she had her keys, she unlocked the door and let herself out into the cold darkness, closing the door quietly behind her.

She picked her way carefully through the garden, and as she entered the small wooded lot that gave way to a field, its stubbled grasses frozen and stiff, she swung the coat over her shoulders. As she slipped her arms into the sleeves, she realized that she had picked up Emma's new red woolen coat in the dark by mistake.

She checked the pockets and, finding only a handkerchief, walked on. We can switch the coats back at the weekend, she thought. Emma'll figure out what's happened. And anyway, it might be fun to wear her coat this week, even if it is a little big.

Because of Emma's fear that the nature of their relationship might be discovered, she insisted that Alys park her car in the lane behind the field at the back of the cottage, never in front.

Alys made her way across the frozen field, came to the verge of the road, and reached in her pocket for her keys.

As she stepped out into the road, keys in hand, she caught a glimpse of movement out of the corner of her eye and then was caught in the blinding glare of headlights. She felt, rather than saw, the car speeding toward her, and before she could react, it was upon her.

She caught a shadowy glimpse of the driver, hunched over the steering wheel, a dark cap pulled down over staring eyes.

Suspended in horrified disbelief at what was happening to her, she felt herself being lifted into the air and carried along on top of the car. It drove on for a few metres, for a few terrifying seconds, as it slowed and then came to a stop. She heard the sound of a car door opening and then felt rough, invisible hands pulling her off the bonnet and throwing her to the ground. Through the unreality she tried to see who was doing this to her, but it was too dark and happening too quickly. As suddenly as it had begun, it was over. The car door slammed shut as the vehicle sped off, leaving her in a crumpled heap by the side of the road.

She lay on her side, shaken and stunned, trying to remain calm. I've been hit, she told herself. Can I stand up?

She tried to pull her legs up toward her chest, but through the excruciating pain she realized that they wouldn't move.

As a rising sense of fear enveloped her, she became aware of the sharp prick of tiny stones on her face. She placed her hand under her cheek and felt a sob escape her.

Oh God, she thought. Is this how I die? Alone, here, in the dark? I can't. I can't. If I can hang on until it's light, someone will come by. It's going to be fine. It will be all right. It's almost morning. Someone will come. Someone will find me.

Emma stirred in her sleep. She swept her hand across the cool sheets where Alys had lain and moved over into the space. Waking slowly and remembering, she turned on the bedside lamp. She held Alys's gift, feeling the weight and coolness of it. She looked at the clock. She'll be well on her way by now, she thought. I'll see her at the weekend. I'll keep busy and the time will go quickly. It won't be long.

Alys saw the light in the upstairs window and cried out. How long? How long have I been here? Is she getting up? Emma, come to the window. Oh, why doesn't somebody help me? And then a welcome warmth surged through her as the crushing pain gave way to merciful darkness.

Five

Remember what I told you—no matter what happens, I will always love you.

A

Penny sighed, blew her nose, and added the tissue to the little pile on the sofa beside her. Then she scrunched them all up into a little ball, placed the soggy mess on the end table, and lay down on the sofa, the last letter in her hand.

So, Emma and Alys had been much more than friends. They'd been lovers and deeply in love.

She felt a wild and wide range of emotions. Immense sadness that Emma should have lost the one she loved, and great compassion that she should have had to live out the rest of her life alone, carrying what must have been an enormous, intense emotional burden.

But most of all Penny felt hurt and confused. She had known Emma for more than twenty years and had never heard of this Alys Jones. Not once had Emma mentioned her. Not one time. You think you know someone, she thought, but you don't. You can't, not really, not completely, because you can never know what went before—who she was before you tumbled into her life, with all your own emotional baggage and youthful dreams. And what of Emma? What must it have been like for her living with that enormous sexual secret all those years, unable to share it. And having to live day by day, never knowing who had robbed her of the one person she loved.

Penny picked up the bunch of tissues, along with the cup of cold tea and took them to the kitchen. As she set the cup in the sink, she was grateful to Victoria for leaving everything so clean and tidy. The dishes had been washed and set out on the counter to dry. Her gaze wandered to the Welsh dresser, and she walked over and stood in front of it looking at the tea set. She picked up a cup and, holding it by the handle, admired the delicate pattern of violets. Violets. A violet ribbon holding the letters. A bank of violets in the paintings. The paperweight she'd noticed yesterday in Emma's bedroom with its little purple flowers.

As she stood in the old-fashioned kitchen, she realized that she hadn't inherited just Emma's home. She'd also inherited all the secrets that went with it. And to live in the cottage, she'd have to peel away all the layers of pain that hid and protected the secrets until she uncovered the darkest one of all.

She replaced the cup on the shelf, sighed, and looked at her watch. Deciding it was not too late to ring him, she went in search of her mobile.

"It's me," she said to his voice mail a few minutes later. "I need your help with something. I wonder if you can get some information on a hit-and-run accident for me. Please call me."

"Of course I'm staggered that she was a lesbian and I never realized that," Penny said to Gareth the next afternoon. "You'd think I would have picked up on that, but I didn't. She certainly never made a pass at me, or whatever you'd call it. Never so much as laid a finger on my knee." She looked down at the untouched scone, with its sad little raisins, sitting on a small plate. Idly she picked off a corner, raised it to her lips, then set it down, and pushed the plate away. She looked around the tearoom, with its low, beamed ceiling and whitewashed walls covered with old pictures of the town, platters, small wooden agricultural tools, and brass plates. Normally, afternoon tea in the Ivy was a treat, the warm biscuits sinfully slathered with unsalted butter, a spoonful of strawberry jam, and large dollops of clotted cream, but today, she was starting to think, it might have been a mistake to come.

He covered her hand with his.

"Look," he said. "You're beating yourself up over something that doesn't matter. None of this changes how you feel about her."

He leaned over to her.

"I think the problem is that you're bringing your perspective and your point of view to her life and times. She was much older than you. She came from a different time, when it

47

wasn't okay to be homosexual. And I use that word deliberately because nobody was gay back then. Think about it. She was a schoolteacher in a small Welsh town! She couldn't have been open about her relationship. It had to be a secret." He thought for a moment, and then added, "It had to be a very big, dark secret. Homosexuality wasn't even legal in this country until the late sixties. Well, that was for men, I don't know about women."

Penny started and withdrew her hand.

"That's right," Gareth continued. "Nineteen sixty-seven or sixty-eight. And remember, her sensibilities would have been different. She might have been confused or even ashamed by her feelings. Who knows?"

"But the one thing that really comes across in those letters," said Penny, "is how much they loved each other. Really, it's to be envied, having that kind of love in your life. So sad the way it ended, and that's why I want to know everything I can about how her partner died."

He couldn't resist smiling at her. "Partner! Emma'd probably be rolling over in her grave if she heard you call her that."

"Well, what then?" said Penny. "Lover? I don't think she'd be too comfortable with that, either. Girlfriend?"

Gareth took a sip of his tea, replaced the cup in its saucer, and glanced at his watch.

"Sorry, love, but I've got to get over to Conwy by seven to help out at a community policing meeting. Tell me how I can help. What would you like me to do?"

Penny leaned forward.

"It's about this hit-and-run accident." She reached into her bag, pulled out her new notebook, and flipped over a few pages.

"Let me see. Here, it is. Alys Jones, killed in a hit-and-run accident, December 1970."

She looked at him expectantly.

"Well?"

"And the rest of it?" he asked.

"The rest of what?"

"Well, there are two big questions to be answered. First, where did it happen, and second, why do you want to know? I have a bad feeling you're going down that road again."

She gave him a flirty smile.

"The sleuth road."

She laughed.

"Of course I am! What would you expect? This accident affected a woman who was a dear friend of mine for years and whose house I'm living in. Something bad happened in her life, and I need to know what it was."

Gareth nodded.

"Well, let me give you a bit of advice. If you want to find out how she died, find out how she lived. Who her friends were, where she went, who she worked with. Start there, and everything else will follow."

He gave her a meaningful look.

"Of course, she may have been hit by a stranger, so none of that will matter. And you do realize, of course, that all this would have been thoroughly investigated at the time. I expect the police put a lot of their resources into it. But if you insist . . ."

Penny nodded.

"Find out how she lived," she repeated. She brightened. "Thanks, Gareth. That makes sense."

She reached for her pen and added an item to her lengthy "to do" list. Then she, too, looked at her watch.

"Don't think you're the only one with places to go. We've got evening customers arriving soon, so I'd best be off as well."

She wiped her hands on the napkin, set it down beside her plate, and reached for her purse.

"Put that away," said Gareth. "My treat. You can buy me a drink later this week. How about Thursday?"

"Great," said Penny. "You can call me later and let me know what time. The Leek and Lily is it?"

Gareth nodded, and together they left the ivy-covered tearoom beside the three-arched bridge. Gareth waved on his way to the car park, and Penny trotted off over the bridge headed for her manicure shop, where Victoria was waiting for her.

A few minutes later she pushed open the door to the tidy manicure shop she had opened some years ago and built up into a thriving business. Victoria emerged from the small preparation room at the back, carrying a small bowl and a pitcher of hot water.

"Oh, it's you," she said. "I thought you were Alwynne arriving early for her appointment. Well, it's a good job you're here now. I expect she'll be in any minute."

"Alwynne Gwilt's got an appointment?" Penny asked.

"Yes," replied Victoria. "You'd do well to stay on top of our business here, Penny! You're coasting these days, and you have to be more plugged in!"

Penny accepted the reprimand with a nod.

"You're right, I better had," she agreed. "I think it's all the upheaval of moving into the cottage."

"Not to mention another distraction." Victoria set down the bowl and pitcher. "Right, well, I've tidied everything up. You're fully booked tonight. Three appointments. I'm not going to stay, but there is something I want to discuss with you, so we'll have to talk soon."

Victoria pulled on a light jacket and opened the door. As she was just about to step out, Alwynne Gwilt appeared on the threshold. They exchanged pleasantries and Alwynne entered.

"Oh, Penny," she said. "I can't tell you how convenient the evening hours are. I bet you'll double your business!"

She took a seat at the table and held out her hands. Penny picked up her left hand and looked critically at her jagged nails.

"What on earth have you been doing to yourself, Alwynne? They look as if you've been breaking rocks with them!"

"I know." Alwynne sighed. "We're putting up a new display at the museum and I was picking away at staples." She looked at Penny. "You're right. I should have taken a few moments to get the right tools."

"Well, you can cut yourself, too, doing things like that," said Penny. "Probably not a good idea. What's the new display about?"

Alwynne looked after the local museum, housed in the old almshouses. Over the years she had put together creative exhibits showing the homefront during World War II; local farmers and their animals, including horse-drawn drays; and one that had attracted a lot of attention—buildings no longer here, including the old town hall.

"Oh, it's set to open in mid-September, so it's about schoolchildren. And that reminds me. I wanted to ask you to be sure to donate anything you find in Emma's cottage that we should have for our archives. Don't throw anything out! Just put it in a pile and I'll go through it. Even old receipts can be useful to us because they show what things used to cost. Personally, I'm very partial to anything written up in old money. I do miss those days of guineas and ten bob notes."

She smiled at Penny and turned her head slightly sideways.

"You haven't thrown out anything, have you?"

"Well, I did donate some old books and jigsaw puzzles to the charity shop, but I think I know what you're after, and no, I won't toss that kind of thing out."

Penny reached for her scissors.

"Alwynne, you've made such a mess here I'm going to have to trim them all right down to try to get them even, and then you can grow them all out at the same time."

Alwynne looked down at her hands and turned the right one over so she could see the nails.

"Well, I guess so," she agreed. "Still, I'd like to have a bit of polish on them today."

"Of course," said Penny, "but I wouldn't recommend anything too loud or obvious."

A kind woman in her fifties with a cheerful bustle about her, Alwynne nodded.

"By the way, how are you getting on with clearing out Emma's things? She lived in that cottage for donkey's years and there has to be tons of stuff. She probably has lots of photos from her school-teaching days, and I'd love to see what's there for my new exhibit. She might have photos of people we know when they were schoolchildren."

52

"I haven't come across any school photos yet," said Penny, "but if I do, I'll let you know."

She put Alwynne's hand back in the soaking bowl and reached for the other hand.

"There's something I'd like to ask you," she said. "Have you ever heard of Alys Jones? She was a local artist, sister of Jones the solicitor. Alys died in a hit-and-run accident in 1970."

Penny met Alywnne's eyes.

"Hmm. It's a big family, that one, but fairly prominent. Of course, with a name like Jones in these parts, you'd expect most of them to be related. We might have some material in the archives, but I can't say offhand"—and recognizing her little pun, Alwynne lifted her hand from the soaking bowl and gave a little laugh—"exactly what. But if you give me a few days, I'll have a look and see what we've got."

"That would be wonderful," said Penny. "Tell you what, can you come round on Friday after dinner for a drink or a coffee, and tell us what you've found out? I'll ask Victoria to join us."

"Right," said Alwynne. "I expect you'd like me to see if there are any photos of her. You know, at the time, while we're living the moment, people don't realize how significant their photos are, but to us at the museum, they're treasures. Most of the photos we get are of people, of course, but I like looking beyond the people to see the material details and settings. Tells us all kinds of things about daily life. What their shoes looked like, the kind of food on the table, that sort of thing. There are even photos with a television in the background, and sometimes you can figure out what they were watching! You'd be surprised at the number of Christmas photos of Gran in a pointy paper hat with the queen on the telly in the background!"

The two women laughed.

"I never thought of that," said Penny, thinking of the photo of Emma with the puppy in the garden. "But look, any Emma photos I come across I'll certainly consider for the museum's archives."

She thought for a moment.

"What's been your best exhibit or most memorable, do you think?"

"Well, a couple of years ago, we had an exhibit of rural life, and every photo had a horse in it. That went over really well and it was definitely one of my favourites. People seemed to really enjoy seeing all those images of life the way it used to be—a slower, friendlier time."

She paused for a moment.

"And the great thing was that some of the people who came to the exhibit actually remembered the names of the horses but not the people. 'That was old what's-his-name who used to work for the dairy,' they'd say, 'Oh, and look, there's Daisy. She was a lovely mare. So gentle with the children.' That sort of thing.

"Of course," she went on, "the pace was different then. Seemed there was more time to enjoy things. Nowadays, it's all go."

Penny nodded. "I know what you mean. We all seem to take on too much."

She thought of the huge project the new spa would no doubt turn out to be—hoovering up enormous amounts of time and endless sums of money. She hoped it would be worth it.

"You know," agreed Alwynne, "that's one reason I enjoy the Stretch and Sketch club so much. I know I'm not that great an artist, but I really welcome the time spent outdoors just being quiet and having the opportunity to relax and do something I enjoy. I always try to make one good decision while I'm out there, even if it's just what I'm going to wear the next day. Or have for dinner."

Penny smiled. A few years ago she had started a friendly group of amateur artists who went out together once a month to ramble and paint. Earlier in the year, Alwynne had taken some photos that had proved helpful in identifying a killer.

"And sometimes," Penny reminded her, "you do some real good on your expeditions!"

Alwynne laughed. A pleasant, down-to-earth, middle-aged woman with a strong streak of practicality and resourcefulness, she took life as she found it. "Anyway," Penny reassured her, "I'll look out for your photos."

"Good. Now, what colour should I have? You choose, Penny."

Six

"Morning, Sergeant."

Sgt. Bethan Morgan looked up from her desk and smiled at her superior officer.

"Morning, sir."

"Good to have you back," Davies replied, as he hung his coat on the hook behind the door. Then, turning to face her, he pointed at the papers covering her desk. "Leave those for now," he said, "and come into my office. There's something I'd like to discuss with you. But before we get into it, why don't we go and grab a coffee?"

After a trip to the canteen, they settled in Davies' office, and he pulled out his notebook as Bethan did the same.

"Now, Sergeant," he began, "as you know, Penny's moved into Emma Teasdale's old cottage, and something has happened.

She's discovered that a close friend of the woman she inherited the cottage from was killed in 1970. Hit-and-run accident. Took place just behind the cottage. The person who did it was never caught."

Bethan felt a stirring of professional excitement. In her early thirties, she was intuitive and ambitious. Her willingness to put in long hours, combined with her solid, reliable work, was attracting attention in all the right places.

"What would you like me do?"

"Well," Davies replied, "as you might have expected, Penny's decided she's going to look into this accident. At first, I wasn't too keen, but now that I've had a chance to think it over, I'm starting to warm to the idea. Sometimes, stirring things up helps uncover new evidence that can breathe new life into a cold case." He took a sip of his lukewarm coffee. "People remember things that didn't seem important at the time and come forward. The phone call. The unlocked door. Something that went missing just a few days before. The car that drove past. Or maybe something's been niggling away at them for years, and realizing they're not getting any younger, they decide to do the right thing and get things off their chest. We had that case a few years back, before your time, when a man in his forties dropped into the station out of the blue one day to tell us he'd seen his uncle murder his aunt. He was about eight at the time, and after all these years, he didn't want to keep his uncle's dirty little secret any longer."

"I did hear something about that," Bethan said. "Do you really think Penny will be able to dig up anything?"

"She's got a knack for seeing the significance in the small details most of us overlook, and I expect she'll bring her friends in on it, so who knows? They might even have resources we don't. Besides, how much trouble can a little group of well-meaning, middle-aged ladies get into?"

As a knowing smile filled with the promise of irony began to form at the corners of Bethan's lips, he groaned.

"Oh, God, don't tell me. Famous last words.

"Anyway, what I'd like you to do is go through the files and pull everything you can on this case. The victim's name was Alys Jones." He spelled the first name.

"Then, put together a proper briefing for them at Penny's cottage. Call Penny and see what time would suit her. Bring a large map, a whiteboard, and some photos and go over everything, so they know as much as we can tell them. Make it look official, but keep it informal, if you know what I mean." He thought for a moment and then added, "and make sure the photos aren't too graphic. We don't want to be upsetting anybody."

He tapped his desk with his finger.

"Let me know who's there and how you get on."

"That'll be fine, Mrs. Lloyd," said Victoria. "Right, we'll see you then." She put the phone down and walked over to the worktable where Penny was applying the topcoat to a client's manicure.

"Penny, that was Mrs. Lloyd. She wanted to know if she could come in earlier tomorrow. I checked the book and switched her for a morning appointment."

Penny nodded as she helped her client gather up her handbag and shopping.

"There you go," she said. "Do be careful, as your nails will be a bit tacky for the next hour or so." With a professional smile, she opened the door, watched as the woman stepped out onto the pavement and turned toward the town square, and only then gently closed the door.

She turned toward Victoria.

"Right. How about a coffee? I'll put the kettle on."

"We have a few minutes," said Victoria, "and there's something I wanted to discuss with you. Let's sit over here."

They sat side by side in the client waiting chairs, and Victoria turned to Penny.

"I'm really excited about the new spa," she said, "and I think this would be a great time to make a few changes," she began.

"Oh, right," said Penny, turning her head slightly. "Here we go!"

"No." Victoria laughed. "It's not bad. I just think that we might be a bit too old here, and we're not tapping into that youth market you hear so much about these days."

She paused.

"Go on," Penny prompted. "I'm interested and I'm listening."

"Well, I was thinking, what if we took on a young person to help out? And especially when we expand the operation, we're going to need someone. I thought someone who's just left school, maybe."

"Have you got somebody special in mind?"

"Well, Eirlys, the daughter of the family I stayed with when I came back to Llanelen, asked me if there might be something here for her. I thought she could perhaps come in

60

on busy days, and then, if she likes it, she could take a training course in Conwy in manicures and pedicures and be available to help you. And once word got round that she was here, maybe more younger girls would want to come here."

Penny thought for a moment.

"She doesn't have any tattoos or body piercings, does she? I can tell you that our older, preferred clientele, like Mrs. Lloyd, say, wouldn't want someone here with bits of metal hanging off their eyebrows."

Victoria shook her head.

"And she won't want to bring in tanning, will she? Absolutely no tanning. I don't want to hear one word about it, and I mean that. It's unhealthy."

"No, there'll never be tanning," agreed Victoria.

"Well, I suppose we could invite her in for a chat," said Penny. "No harm in that, is there?"

"No harm at all."

"And we'll have to make it clear that making tea and coffee will be part of her duties. For some reason, young people today seem to think making the tea is beneath them. You don't think she'd mind doing that, do you?"

Victoria shook her head.

"If she'd been here now we could have had that coffee ten minutes ago. And we'll have to show her how to make it properly. I don't want her thinking she can get away with using hot water out of the tap. That's why we have a kettle. And speaking of which . . ."

Victoria laughed and was about to reply when the phone rang. She answered it.

"Oh, hello, Bethan, yes, she's right here."

61

"Hello!" said Penny, taking up the phone. "Glad you're back." She listened for a few moments and then clutched Victoria by the arm and gently pulled her over to her.

"Just let me ask Victoria. I'm sure she'd want to be there."

"Friday night," said Penny. "Can you come over for dinner with Bethan? She's going to talk to us about the case."

"Absolutely," said Victoria. "Is she coming for dinner?"

Penny nodded and returned to the phone.

"Victoria's going to make dinner. Right. Come about six," she said. "Great, see you then."

Penny hung up the phone and then looked at her friend.

"What?"

"Why did you say I was going to make dinner?"

"Aren't you? I thought you were offering!"

"No, I was just asking!"

"Well"—Penny shrugged—"if you don't want to, that's all right. Not a problem. We'll just get some take-away. Maybe Thai. Bethan likes that."

"I suppose I could do my tarragon chicken," muttered Victoria, "but I must say, you really should have asked me first."

"I'm sorry," said Penny. "Tell you what. I'll make a really nice salad to go with it."

Victoria let out a small snort.

"You'll buy a bag of shredded lettuce from the supermarket, more like. Anyway, it'll be good to see Bethan again. She's a sweetheart."

Penny nodded. "She said she's found the old evidence boxes and that the files even contain photographs. Oh, and speaking

62

of photographs, Alwynne is coming over, too, to bring whatever she's found at the museum. It should be an interesting evening. Is there anyone else we should invite?"

"Not sure. Let me think about it."

The door opened and the next client arrived.

Looking at her tightly permed grey hair, sensible shoes, pleated skirt, and worn leather handbag, Penny realized Victoria was right. *We do need some young energy around here. Practically everybody who comes in here is middle aged or older, and it's starting to get very dreary. Not only that, when this lot are no longer able to come to the salon, there'll be no customers left. And looking ahead to the new spa business, these elderly women are definitely not the sort to pay up for a day's pampering. We're going to need a whole new clientele.*

She smiled at her client and invited her to sit down.

"I'll be right with you," she said. "Just got to get your soaking bowl."

And then an awful thought occurred to her.

"Sorry," she added, "just need a quick word with Victoria."

Victoria looked up from the small desk where she was starting to sort receipts into three small piles.

"Hmm?"

"About the new young person who's coming here. Be sure to tell her there isn't a hope in hell that we'll give house room to those hideous fake acrylic nails!"

She thought for a moment.

"What did you say her name is again?"

"Eirlys. Here, let me write it down for you." Victoria handed Penny a slip of paper. "That's the correct spelling of it, but phonetically, it would be Ire-less." She smiled as Penny repeated the name softly to herself. "You know what Welsh spelling is like! But it's a rather pretty girl's name, actually. It's Welsh for 'snowdrop.'"

Seven

Evelyn Lloyd, the town's former postmistress, had been one of Penny's steadiest customers for years. She always came in for her manicure on a Thursday, her bridge night, as she liked her nails to look their best as she dealt cards or reached across the table to play the dummy's hand.

"Oh, good morning, Penny," she said as she pushed her way through the door. "So good of you to take me earlier. I have a friend of mine from the old post office days coming for lunch today and wanted to get my manicure out of the way so we could spend the afternoon together."

Mrs. Lloyd put down her shopping and looked around, taking in the nail polishes neatly arranged by colour, ranging from pale pinks to vivid reds and brilliant burgundies.

"Well, what's this I hear about you and Victoria going into

business together? I do hope this expansion won't mean higher prices. And as I've suggested many times, you really ought to offer senior discounts. Think of all the new customers that would bring in!"

"Yes, Mrs. Lloyd, you might be right," said Penny diplomatically as she sat down opposite her client. She picked up Mrs. Lloyd's left hand, unwrapped a new emery board, and started shaping her nails.

Victoria and Penny had discussed whether they should ask Mrs. Lloyd if she remembered anything about the Jones hit-and-run accident. Victoria had figured she would remember plenty and thought it would be a good idea; Penny wouldn't hear of it.

"You know what she's like," Penny had said. "She'll try to take this over. Emma was my friend and I want to do this my way."

So they'd left it at that, with Penny finally agreeing that if they needed Mrs. Lloyd's local knowledge later, they'd consult her then. In the meantime, they knew there was little hope that she wouldn't get wind that they were looking into the case.

When she had finished shaping Mrs. Lloyd's nails, Penny brought out a small basin of steaming soaking water, which she set down on her worktable. "Right, Mrs. Lloyd, let's be having you."

Mrs. Lloyd gingerly dipped the tips of her fingers in the basin and then quickly withdrew them.

"Oh, why does the water always have to be so hot?" she complained, making an elaborate display of curling up her fingers.

"So it will soften up your cuticles," replied Penny. "Is it really too hot? If so, I can cool it down."

"Oh, I guess I can tolerate it," grumbled Mrs. Lloyd as she placed her fingers in the bowl once more. "It seems to have cooled off a bit." She brightened. "What colour should we have today? Do you know, I fancy something with a little drama!"

"So tell me about your friend from the post office," Penny asked conversationally. "What will the two of you be getting up to, then?"

"We're going to Llandudno to shop and have a nice tea at Badgers," Mrs. Lloyd replied. "And then, as tonight is my regular bridge game, she'll make up the table, since one of our players has not been very well of late."

"Oh, I am sorry to hear that. I hope she'll be better soon. Still, it's nice that your friend can stand in."

"Yes, it is," Mrs. Lloyd agreed. "And independent women like you have a lot to thank my friend for."

"We do?"

"Oh, yes." Mrs. Lloyd nodded. "Bunny, well, we call her Bunny because she was always so quick on her rounds, but her real name is Mavis. Anyway, Bunny was one of the first lady post office van drivers in this area. All over the valley in her van, she was, with the deliveries. And always right on time, too. Had to be, see. Had to show the powers that be that women could do the job just as well as the men. So it was women like her, in all kinds of jobs, that made it possible for your generation to do the things you've done."

Mrs. Lloyd's eyes slid over to the rack of nail polishes. "What colour did we decide on today? Or did we? I'd like something with some depth to it." She pointed to a bright red. "How about that one?"

"I don't think you want that one," Penny said. "It's got that shimmer in it that you don't like."

"Oh, right. Well, something else then, but the same kind of colour."

Penny got up, selected three from the shelf, and offered them to Mrs. Lloyd. "How about one of these?" She held one up. "This one will look very nice on you."

Mrs. Lloyd turned the bottle over and read the name.

"Deer Valley Spice. Well, I have no idea what that means, but it's just what I had in mind!"

Just before six on Friday evening an unmarked police car drove slowly along the lane leading to Penny's cottage. It pulled up outside the front door and Bethan got out. She walked around to the passenger side, opened the door, and pulled out a large whiteboard. Carrying it to one side, she picked her way carefully along the path that led to the front door. Leaning the board up against the building, she returned to the car and a few moments later set down an oversized envelope beside the whiteboard. Then she rang the doorbell.

Her face broke into a wide grin when Penny, one hand outstretched, opened the door to her.

"Come in, come in," Penny greeted her. "Here, let me give you a hand with those things." She put her hand on the envelope. "I can't wait to see what you've got in here. I haven't been able to think of anything else all day!"

She led Bethan into the sitting room and invited her to sit down.

"Victoria's making us something really special for our tea, and it shouldn't be long."

Bethan smiled as she looked around the room. Much of the clutter was gone, and Penny had rearranged the furniture to open up the space. Penny pointed to a blank wall where two large easels had been set up.

"I thought you could put your whiteboard on them, if they're sturdy enough," she said. "What do you think?"

"Hmm. I think that arrangement will work for tonight," Bethan said, "but if you want to keep the board up and we really start working with it, we might need to make it more secure so we can write on it and tape things to it."

Penny nodded eagerly and then turned as Victoria emerged from the kitchen, wearing a large white apron with a tea towel draped over her shoulder.

"Hi, Bethan, love," she said warmly. "It's so nice to see you again. Has Penny offered you a drink yet?"

"No, not yet," replied Bethan, "but I'm sure she was just about to. I'll just have a tonic water or a ginger ale, please."

"Right you are," said Penny. "Are you on duty?"

"We couldn't really decide that. I don't think so, but it feels like it. Anyway, I have to drive back to Llandudno tonight, so from that point of view, have to give the wine a miss. This time."

Penny nodded and headed off to the kitchen to fetch Bethan's drink.

"Here you go," she said a few moments later, handing her a

frosty glass of tonic water. "There was even a slice of lemon going spare." She looked eagerly at the whiteboard.

"Are you going to set it up now and show us what you have?" she asked.

"No, I am not! We'll do that after dinner, which smells delicious, by the way. I haven't seen you and Victoria in ages, and I've been looking forward to this meal all day, so we're going to save the business part until after!"

Penny gave a little whimper of disappointment.

"You two can sit down," Victoria called from the kitchen. "I'll just bring things through."

A few minutes later they were enjoying their meal of tarragon chicken with rice and steamed vegetables.

"This looks wonderful," exclaimed Bethan as she reached across the table to take the bowl of vegetables from Penny.

"It would have been even better," said Victoria with a pointed look in Penny's direction, "with a salad. But someone seems to have forgotten it."

"Oh, that reminds me," said Penny, jumping up. "You're right, I did forget the salad, but I picked up fresh bread rolls at the bakery. I'll just pop them in the oven for a few minutes. Be right back."

"Alywnne is coming over for dessert and coffee and to hear your presentation," Victoria told Bethan. "She's also meant to be bringing what she's dug up on Alys Jones." She lowered her voice. "Penny is going to be totally obsessed with this until she finds out what happened. She'll be like a terrier with her head down a rabbit hole."

Bethan nodded.

"What were you saying?" asked Penny as she slid back into her seat and set down a basket of warm rolls.

"Victoria was just saying Alywnne's coming over," Bethan replied and, with a sharp nod in Penny's direction, added, "let's leave it there for now. Let me enjoy my dinner in peace. Now then, tell me about your plans for the new spa. I hope you'll be offering massages."

"Massages, possibly," said Penny. "Tanning, absolutely not." Victoria nodded.

"We'll be going over the building in a few days. It's been empty so long it's going to need masses of work, but from the outside it has wonderful potential. I'm not sure about all the uses it's been put to over the years, but when I was a girl and used to visit Llanelen, it was a men's hostel. I heard somewhere that in the old days it was a coaching inn. Anyway, it's a beautiful stone building and I'm really looking forward to seeing the inside of it."

Bethan laid down her fork and sighed.

"Would you like seconds?" Victoria asked. "There's lots more."

"No, thanks," said Bethan, holding up a hand. "But it was delicious. I don't get home-cooked meals very often, so I really enjoyed it. It was a treat." She smiled at Victoria in a satisfied way that made her look like a teenager.

They sat for a moment contemplating the remains of the meal. When Victoria stood up and reached for the platter of leftover chicken, Penny and Bethan exchanged quick glances.

"I'll clear this away," said Victoria, catching their meaning, "while the two of you get on with it. Penny's dying to see what you've got."

"Right," said Penny, jumping up. "What would you like me to do?"

"Help me make sure the whiteboard is steady," said Bethan, "and then I'll put up a few photos."

As they lifted the board onto the easels, a knock on the front door brought Victoria from the kitchen. "I'll get it," she said, setting a teapot on the table as she walked by. "It'll be Alwynne, no doubt."

It was, but she wasn't alone.

"Hello, we met out front and thought we'd come in together," Davies said as he and Alwynne entered. "Hope you don't mind, but I thought I'd just listen in. Don't mind me. I'll just sit quietly at the back and not get in anyone's way. It's Bethan's show."

"Actually, you can help us move the furniture, if you would," said Penny, when the greetings were over. "Let's push the sofa against this wall and put the display here so we can all see it properly."

"Tea and chocolate cake on the table for those who want it!" called Victoria.

"I'd love a cup," said Davies. "Shall I be mother?"

"Yes, do." Victoria laughed. "Here are the spoons."

A few minutes later Bethan took her place in front of the whiteboard. Penny sat on the sofa, with her notebook open on her lap. Victoria and Alwynne sat to one side, on chairs taken from the dining room, and Davies leaned against the wall, balancing a cup of tea in one hand on a saucer he held in the other.

"Right," said Bethan, glancing at the papers she was holding. "Let me begin by explaining what happened to Alys Jones in the early morning hours of Saturday, December 5, 1970.

"Sometime not long before daybreak, Alys Jones was apparently on her way to her vehicle, an MG, which had been parked just here," she said, pointing to a map. "In those days the road was unpaved, and the surrounding area was mainly fields, but now, of course, the area has been built up and includes the housing estate just behind the cottage where we are now."

She pointed toward Penny's back door.

"The police received a distress call about six thirty A.M. from a local resident, who had discovered the victim lying in the road. When emergency services reached her, her vital signs were very weak and she died en route to hospital.

"She was the victim of a hit-and-run accident, and the perpetrator was never caught. We don't know if it was an accident or if she had been deliberately targeted. However, while there was nothing in her past to indicate this was anything other than a tragic accident, the investigation revealed that the driver had made no effort to avoid her. There was no indication of braking or swerving, and for that reason, the accident was regarded as suspicious."

She paused and looked from one still, focused face to the next. Davies took a slow sip of tea. The clink of china as he set the cup back on its saucer seemed magnified in the silence.

"Of course, forensics weren't as good then as they are today," Bethan continued, "and evidence might have been available that, looked at today, could reveal something. But measurements were taken at the time, and it was determined

73

that the point of impact was here." She pointed to an **X** on the map. "However, the body was found lying some ten metres farther along the road. We aren't sure if the victim managed to somehow make her way that distance, or"—she paused for effect and to allow her small audience to prepare themselves— "if the body had been caught and carried along on the car and then fell off. From her injuries, it didn't look as if the body had been dragged."

"What about the car or vehicle that hit her?" Victoria asked. "Was it ever located?"

"No. The local garages were notified and asked to be on the lookout for someone bringing in a damaged car for repairs, but nothing turned up."

After a moment's silence, she continued.

"House-to-house inquiries were also conducted, including, of course, this one. No one heard or saw anything."

She looked at Penny.

"Would you like to come up and take a closer look at the photos?"

The others watched respectfully as Penny approached the board. She peered at the grainy black-and-white photos for a moment, and then Bethan pointed at one.

"Start with this one, Penny," she said. "This photo is a general look at the scene and will give you an idea of where everything was in relation to everything else. So you can see her car still parked just here." She pointed to the MG. "And the body was found farther along, about here." Bethan's finger slid along the photo and stopped.

Penny scanned all the photos, then looked inquiringly at Bethan, who shook her head.

"No, no photos of her here. She was found alive and the priority was to get her to casualty."

"Now many questions remain unanswered," Bethan continued when the group had settled back in their chairs. "We know the victim had a family connection to this town, but we don't know what she was doing here at that time. Why she was where she was at that time of day, if you know what I mean."

Penny rubbed her hands together as if she were experiencing a slight chill and glanced at Davies.

"I think I can answer that," she said. "Alys had spent the night here, in this cottage, with Emma."

No one said anything.

"And even though their relationship was not platonic, I'm having a hard time trying to understand why Emma didn't tell the police that Alys had stopped here that night. That piece of information might have helped with the inquiry. And surely, she would have wanted to know who did this."

Alwynne looked startled, as if she had just realized the implications of what Penny had said.

"Not platonic? Are you telling me that Emma was a lesbian?" she asked. Penny nodded.

"Well, Penny, that's why she couldn't say anything to the police! Even now, there'd probably be lots of folks in this town who wouldn't want a lesbian teaching their children. But back then?" She gave a little snort and shook her head. "The poor thing. What must it have been like for her, all these years?" And then, as a new thought came to her, she sighed.

"She wouldn't be too happy even today, knowing that her

secret is out. I don't suppose we could keep this quiet, could we? Just amongst ourselves, like?" She looked from one to the other and, when no one answered, reached into her large, over-stuffed purse.

"Is it my turn, now? I managed to dig up some family history and found an interesting photo for you, Penny."

Bethan and Alwynne changed places. Alwynne turned her back on her small audience while she taped a black-and-white photo to the whiteboard.

"Now then," she began and pointed at the photo. "This is the Jones family, taken at a picnic, oh, sometime in the 1940s, best we can tell. I do so wish people would write the date on the back of their photos. Anyway, the parents here are Elwyn and Myfanwy and you can see the three children. There's the twins, Alys and Richard, probably about ten, and the baby is their younger brother, Alun."

"Twins!" exclaimed Penny. "Alys and Richard were twins?"

Alywnne looked confused.

"Yes, of course they were. I am so sorry—I thought you knew. Richard was absolutely lost when she was killed. Took it very hard, he did. They always say twins have that very special bond."

Penny settled back in the sofa with a small sigh. She exchanged a quick glance with Gareth and then turned her attention back to Alwynne.

"Anyway, the family had a little farm just outside Llanelen and made a fairly reasonable living. But the mother was a great one for education, even back then, and insisted that her children would be educated, and so they were. And they all made something of themselves. Alys went away to art school and had a good teaching job when she died and, by all accounts, was coming into her own as an artist. Richard became a solicitor, as you know, and the baby, Alun, became a vet. I think he really would have preferred to take up farming like his dad, but he did the next best thing, in his mind. He loves lambing time, does Alun. Practically lives in the fields with the farmers when all that's going on."

"That would be our local vet, then?" said Victoria. "Jones the vet."

"That's right." Alwynne nodded. "He would have been in his early twenties when his sister was killed."

She looked from one to the other.

"That's all I have so far, but I'm sure I can find out more, if you want me to, Penny. I'd like to help."

Penny stood up and went over to her.

"There are so many unanswered questions, and every bit helps." She smiled in Gareth's direction. "We need to find out everything about how she lived."

Soon after the group broke up and began to drift toward the front door. Bethan offered Victoria and Alwynne a ride home, which they gladly accepted, and she steered them toward the car. Davies stayed behind and put his arm around Penny's waist, pulling her to him.

"Do I have to go, too? Please don't send me out into that cold, dark night."

Penny laughed. "It's barely September and it's not that cold or that dark, and yes, you do. I'm not ready yet for that kind of entertaining, but when I am, you'll be the first to know."

Davies kissed her and then reluctantly released her.

"Make it soon."

And then, spotting the large envelope Bethan had left on the floor, propped up against the legs of an easel, he asked rhetorically, "Now have we got everything?"

Following his gaze, Penny started to say something, but Davies held up his hand.

"Yes, we do," he said with a smile. "Well, I'll leave you to it then. Night, love."

And like the others, he disappeared into the late summer night knowing that Penny would be devouring every word in the file before he'd turned the corner.

Eight

"There's nothing like a good breeze on wash day," Bronwyn Evans said to her husband, the rector, the next afternoon as she poured him his second cup of tea.

"Mmm hmm," came a feeble attempt at agreement from behind a magazine.

Then, setting the magazine down beside his plate, he looked fondly at his wife.

"Sorry, darling, you were saying?"

"Oh, I was just on about how nice it is when there's a breeze for the clothes on wash day." She stood up. "Can I get you another piece of cake, dear?"

"No, that was lovely, thanks. I'll just sit here for a bit and finish this article, if that's all right with you. I know you have things you want to get on with. Don't let me hold you up."

She reached over and placed a gentle hand on his shoulder.

"Thomas, after all these years I can tell when you're avoiding working on your sermon for tomorrow. But you'll get it done. You always do."

And leaving him to bask for a moment in her warm smile, she walked to the kitchen, where she picked up the wicker clothes basket that had once belonged to her mother-in-law.

I wonder what they'd have to say about you on the *Antiques Roadshow*, she thought as she hoisted the basket onto her hip, let herself out the back door, and walked to her clothesline at the bottom of the rectory garden.

The rectory, church, and adjoining cemetery were beautifully situated beside the River Conwy. The bright water sparkled in the early afternoon sunshine as small ripples splashed ashore.

Light, cool gusts of wind touched her cheek, and she felt her spirits rise as she set the empty basket down and reached up to the clothesline to begin taking in the laundry.

She pulled the pegs off a fluttering towel and unable to resist, as she did every time she brought in air-dried laundry, held the towel to her nose and breathed in its natural, fresh scent. It brought back happy memories of her childhood and all the years since. As she stood there with the towel pressed against her face, she heard a snuffled, whimpering sound. Lowering the towel, she swiveled her shoulders and looked around. The garden and cemetery were deserted. She folded the towel, placed it in the basket, and took the next one off the line.

The sound came again, a little stronger this time, and she recognized it as a cry for help.

She let the towel fall into the basket and walked into the cemetery, in the direction she thought the sound had come from.

Please make another noise so I can find you, whoever you are, she thought. A moment later, she heard a little whine, and as she stepped behind a large tombstone, she saw it.

Its matted fur clung to slack, malnourished skin. Dark, damp eyes gazed up at her, knowing she was its last chance for survival. She turned and ran back to her clothesline. Without bothering to remove the pegs, she pulled at two more towels, ignoring the *ping! ping!* of the pegs as they released the towels and flew away to land in the grass nearby. Tossing the towels in the basket and quickly adjusting them to make a soft nest, she scooped up the basket and ran back to the shivering dog.

"Here we go," she said as she tenderly lifted the frightened dog into the basket. "Let's be having you." She set its head down slowly and risked a tentative pat that she hoped would be reassuring. As her hand neared its mouth, a small pink tongue reached out and licked her.

Holding back tears and bearing the basket carefully in front of her, she walked back to the rectory as quickly as she could and pushed open the door.

"Thomas! Thomas!" she called.

Responding to the urgency in her voice, Reverend Evans emerged from his study and hurried down the hall toward her.

"What is it, my dear? Are you all right? Has something happened?"

"I'm fine, Thomas," she said impatiently. "But look!"

"You want me to look at the laundry?"

"No! Thomas, look inside the basket."

The rector leaned forward and peered into the fluffy folds of the towels.

"Wherever did you find it?" he asked, then, looking again, added, "What is it, do you think?'

"It's a weak and injured dog, you ninny," his wife replied. "Now you need to call Jones the vet and ask if he can see us immediately and then bring the car round. I'll be waiting out front." A few moments later, she added, "And be sure to bring my handbag with you."

The vet's surgery was crowded, but the receptionist waved them through and a few moments later the rector was setting the basket down on the examination table.

"Well, well," said the vet, as he reached inside. "Let's get you out so we can take a good look at you."

He lifted the shivering animal from the basket and gestured to Reverend Evans to pull the basket out of the way.

Jones held up his stethoscope and set it against the dog's chest. He inclined his head as he listened and then straightened. He ran his hands gently down the dog's side and then felt each limb.

He stood back and crossed his arms.

"This little fellow has been neglected and he's severely malnourished," he said. "But I don't think anything's broken, and with proper care he should be right as rain in no time."

He directed a question to Bronwyn. "How did you come to have him?"

"I found him in the churchyard," she replied, "behind a tombstone. He was very wet. Had he been in the river, do you think?"

The vet nodded. "It's possible, I'm afraid, that someone tried to drown him. There's a bit of rope here attached to his collar. It might have had a weight attached to it. Unfortunately, this is not the first case like this I've seen lately."

"Oh dear Lord," exclaimed the rector. "How on earth could anyone hurt a poor little creature like this?"

"I ask myself that very question every time I see an abused animal," said Jones. "Well, I think we have to figure out what to do next. This dog has been neglected and abused for some time, so there's certainly no point in trying to find the owner, but it won't be difficult finding a permanent home for him."

"I don't suppose you know anyone who'd welcome a little chap into the family, do you?"

The couple looked at each other.

"Well, with our busy schedules we don't really have time to look after a dog," the rector said. "Parish business and all that."

Bronwyn shot him a glance and touched his arm.

"But perhaps we might just take him home with us now and nurse him back to health . . ."

"That's an excellent idea," agreed the vet. "And please bring him back in about a week or so and let me see how he's getting on. And of course, call me if he's not progressing as well as you think he should."

"Should we do anything special for him?" asked Bronwyn. "Food or anything like that?"

"Well, I reckon he's about two years old," said Jones, "so he can manage adult food. Start him off slowly with some high-quality kibble mixed with warm water to soften it, then some rice added. We'll give you some free samples of the right sort of food to get you started. And make sure he always has water available."

The rector placed the basket on the table, and Jones expertly lowered the dog into it. The rector glanced at the dog and then turned to the vet.

"What kind of dog would you say he is?"

"Oh, there's no doubt about that," replied the vet. "He's a cairn terrier. A wee Scottish fellow."

Nine

Victoria had reminded Penny that Eirlys, the daughter of the family with whom she had stayed earlier that year, who was hoping to be taken on as a junior, was coming in for an interview at lunchtime.

Just before noon the door opened and a young woman with long dark hair clipped jauntily on top of her head, leaving a few bobbing, youthful wisps, slipped quietly into the salon. Penny's client turned to see who had just arrived and broke into a broad smile.

"Eirlys, love! It's grand to see you. How are your mum and dad?"

That does it, thought Penny. We're having her.

Forty-five minutes later, with her duties and hours of work explained and a training scheme agreed to, Eirlys bounded happily out of the salon, leaving Victoria and Penny to head upstairs to Victoria's flat for a quick lunch.

"What did I tell you!" exclaimed Victoria as they entered the small, neat sitting room.

"Yes, you were right," Penny agreed. "I could feel the atmosphere change as soon as she walked into the room. Of course, with that gorgeous dark hair and blue eyes, she's a scene stealer."

She made a quick pointing gesture at Victoria. "That's it! Of course! I was trying to think who she reminded me of and it's Catherine Zeta-Jones.

"Anyway, I really hope this works out as well as I think it's going to. Do you know, she even asked me if she could wear a smock, as she thinks it looks more professional. Do you think she might have seen that in a movie?"

"No"—Victoria smiled—"she saw it in a salon in Llandudno. She visited a couple as part of her research so she'd have a better idea of what the job might involve."

"Well, I'm impressed! I give her a lot of credit for that."

"Anyway, I'm famished. Let's get the kettle on and then figure out what we're going to have for lunch."

As they sat down to their sandwiches, Victoria's phone rang.

"Oh, hi, Bronwyn," she said and, after a moment, added, "yes, I did mention the jumble sale to Penny and she's going to do Emma's room very soon and sort out the clothes and things for you."

She tilted her head meaningfully in Penny's direction and then listened for a few moments.

"Really! The cemetery? How lucky that you found him when you did. What did the vet say?"

She listened for a few more minutes and then rang off.

"You'll never guess," she said to Penny.

"No, I probably won't," said Penny, "so you'd better tell me."

"Well, it's just that Bronwyn found a dog in the cemetery. At death's door, he was. So they took him to the vet, and now they're looking after him for a bit. Nursing him back to health. I thought I might go over later and see him."

"Took him to the vet, eh? Do you think they'll be taking him to the vet again?"

"Well, I don't know. I guess it depends on how well the dog . . ." Her voice trailed off. "Oh, I get it. The vet. Alun Jones the vet. That vet."

Penny nodded. "Victoria, that's a brilliant idea that you should look in on the poor dog. And find out if Bronwyn's going back to see the vet, and if she is, let's invite her and Thomas round on Friday evening for a little chat. I think they can help with our investigation. They've got the perfect opportunity to poke around a bit and see if Alun Jones can tell us anything about the accident. He might have heard something."

Victoria nodded. "Not one to miss an opportunity, are you?"

"Right. And there's something else we can ask Thomas to do," Penny continued. "Emma's journals. I really don't want to read them myself, not yet anyway, and who knows? Maybe I never will. But remember a few months back when Thomas agreed to go through one or two when we were looking for background information that we hoped would help in that business about the missing bride? And besides, as a rector, he knows about keeping things confidential, so Emma's secrets, whatever they may be, will be safe with him. So let's ask him to go over the crucial years. Emma might have made notes about people or events that could be helpful to us now."

She paused for a moment and then reached for her note-book. "I wish I could go with you to Bronwyn's. But I can't wait to hear all about the dog."

On Wednesday, Penny and Victoria met the estate agent to go over the riverside property they were considering for conversion into the Llanelen Spa. They considered its location right beside the Red Dragon Hotel a bonus and, if they decided to buy it, planned to approach the hotel owners to discuss redecorating and upgrading rooms for the exclusive use of their out-of-town clients.

"Now I must be honest with you," the estate agent was saying as they studied the outside of the three-storey dark grey stone building, admiring the way it stood its timeless ground against the river. "There isn't much space for parking and that could be a drawback."

"We've thought of that," said Penny, "and we think it could be an advantage. We will encourage our clients to come by train—we can arrange for them to be met at the station. More environmentally friendly and relaxing. No driving!"

The front of the building, which faced the river, featured a small path that led to a few crumbling stairs.

"It's been empty for a long time," the estate agent warned as he unlocked the bright blue door. "Prepare yourselves, and don't expect too much."

The two women glanced at each other, and then Victoria stepped tentatively inside. She found herself in a large entry hall, permeated by an overwhelming smell of damp and decay. Peeling plaster, which had once been painted a vibrant turquoise, hung from the walls exposing thin wood strips. She turned around and motioned for Penny to join her, and the two set off to tour the rooms while the estate agent waited outside, occasionally glancing at his watch.

"What do you think?" asked Penny when they had looked over the building. They knew the building had been on the market with no interest for years and had decided that if they were to move forward with it, Victroria would take the lead on the property development, and once the structural work was done, Penny would oversee the decorating and furnishing.

"If we were to make an offer, I'm sure we'd get it way below asking price. Everyone else sees it as it is, and no one wants it. We see it as it could be, and we do want it. What we'd really be buying is the potential," said Victoria. "It's been abandoned for ages so no surprises. It's about what I expected."

She gestured toward the river. "The location is a huge plus. The land value alone would be a great investment for us. We do it up . . ."

Penny nodded. "Go on."

"Look, let's get the surveyor to go over it and give us a report on the structure. That way, we can get an idea of how sound it is and what would be required. You could then draw up a few sketches of what you think we'd like it to look like, and we can move forward with the work. We'll want to knock down some of the interior walls to open up the space. And put in a really good kitchen. That sort of thing.

"But if you can imagine it with hardwood floors, new walls, beautiful pastel paint colours, really high-end bathrooms with rain forest showers—all the fixtures and fittings . . ."

"Stop!" Penny laughed. "I'm starting to get excited. Next you'll be talking about rose petals and tea lights! Let's do it!"

"And here's another thought," added Victoria. "If they do a good job on this building, they could probably have your cottage done up in no time. You'll be getting, what, a new kitchen, new bathroom, and everything painted and new floors?"

"I've been thinking about that," said Penny. "I'm going to leave it as it is until I find out why Alys Jones died. I think renovating it now will take me too far from Emma and Alys."

She thought for a moment. "No, what I really mean is renovating it now will take them too far away from me. While everything is as they knew it, I can picture them there and feel close to them. When we know what happened to Alys, then I'll be able to get on with the redecorating."

Victoria touched her arm. "And move on. I understand. Oh, and speaking of moving on, I wondered what you'd think of the idea of incorporating a small flat into the spa for me on the top floor? I'll have to move out anyway when we give up the lease on the salon and this way, we'll have someone on the premises all the time. Good idea, yes?"

"Yes, good idea."

"And you know, I also think we could have a reception room. If it were done properly, it could be used for corporate events and maybe even small weddings. We'll have kitchen facilities so we could generate extra income by renting it out."

"Oh, I do like the sound of that," said Penny, adding, "and

we might even be able to offer musical evenings. You could perform."

An accomplished harpist, Victoria had performed in London until her recent move to Llanelen.

Smiling, they rejoined the anxious estate agent. After all this time, could today be my lucky day, he asked himself as he saw them approaching. He almost felt sorry for them. What could two middle-aged women possibly want with a run-down old building like this? Did they have any idea what they'd be taking on? Still, business is business, and in real estate the offers you least expect are often the best ones. Not to mention the only ones.

Penny finished up for the day and said good-bye to Victoria, leaving her to close the shop. As she walked home through the familiar streets, she realized that it was now well into September and she could feel the evenings beginning to draw in. The sun was setting that much sooner now, and it wouldn't be long until she would be getting out her warm clothes, including her favourite sweaters that had been unworn for months, waiting for their time to come again.

The artist in her loved the colours of fall, the rich reds and browns of turning leaves. While Wales did not have the extravagant display of leaf colours she had known as a child in her native Nova Scotia, the ivy on the tea shop did turn a lustrous scarlet and put on a brave show. She thought about Canada from time to time but did not long for it. This had been her home for many years, and in her heart she would always belong here, not there.

As she turned into the little lane that led to her cottage, her thoughts turned again to Alys. What was she like, she wondered. What did her accent sound like? Did she have a favourite fragrance?

She walked through the small front garden to her front door. She had arranged for a neighbourhood boy to start work on the garden after school, and just as Gareth had promised, with the weeds gone and order restored it was looking much better. The pale pink, late-summer roses nodded gently to her as she brushed by them, and she smiled as she put her key in the door.

As she pushed the door open and entered the living room, she sensed the change that had come over the house in the short weeks that she had been there. Gone was the sense of unloved abandonment and loneliness; the house was filling up again with contentment and energy and was slowly starting to take on the personality of its new owner.

Suddenly, Penny was impatient to lay its ghosts to rest. I must find out what happened so I can put this behind me and get on with my life, she thought. She glanced at her watch. The library would be open for another hour. She closed the door again and hurried out.

Seated at the computer, she typed in "Liverpool artists 1960s." There were masses of material on the Merseyside music scene, a little about the poetry scene, but not much about artists. On a different search, there were lots of Alys Joneses but not her Alys Jones. Twenty-five very fast minutes later the banner warning her that her time was almost up crawled along the bottom of the screen. She closed her notebook and stood up.

On the way out, she thanked the librarian and made a mental note that getting her own computer had now risen to the top of her priorities list. She had even heard somewhere that you didn't need to get the Internet cable installed in your home now; you could get a little thing that plugged into your computer and the Internet was instantly available to you. Laptop, she thought. I'll get a laptop and I'll get it right away. I'll ask Bethan what kind to get. She's young and smart—she'll know about things like that. Oh, God, do I feel old and out of it.

But still, she told herself, if she couldn't find what she wanted on the Internet, there was an old-fashioned, low-tech way, and she knew exactly where she had to go to do it.

"Well, Penny," said Mrs. Lloyd the next day at her regular Thursday afternoon manciure, "I hear Eirlys is going to be working here. About time, too! You know I've been telling you for years that you need someone young about the place to liven us all up. Someone on the BBC was saying just this morning that mentorship is the way to go. It helps us view the world through younger eyes and keeps us in touch with what young people are up to.

"Now, in my day," she went on, "things moved much more slowly. But the pace of change these days! You simply can't keep up with it. As you know, I got my mobile phone a few months ago and I do use it for making calls, but apparently I could use it to take photos, send text messages, and all kinds of other things. Send text messages! I ask you—who on earth would I send a text message to?"

Penny nodded as Mrs. Lloyd rambled on. Once she was up and running, there was no stopping her. Penny's thoughts drifted away.

". . . and then," Mrs. Lloyd was continuing, "I'll be going to Llandudno for my usual tea at Badgers. But my friend Bunny from the post office days, the one who came to lunch last week—you'll remember I told you about her—she was suggesting that we might go to the theatre in Manchester and stop overnight at her daughter's home. So I think we'll do that. And no doubt she'll want to come in for a manicure, too, before we go. There! Now I've brought you another customer. It's good to get away every now and then, even for a weekend, don't you think? Brings a different perspective to things."

Penny, who was applying the second coat of Mrs. Lloyd's polish, stopped and, holding the brush in midair, smiled at her.

"Do you know, Mrs. Lloyd, I think you're right, as usual. By the way, how do you like this colour? You're getting a little daring in your choice of colours, I must say."

"Yes, does it seem a little brighter than the usual ones? What's it called, again?"

"Baguette Me Not. It's from the France collection."

"Baguette . . . that reminds me . . . must stop in at the bakery on the way home. I do like a baguette with some Brie and a bit of celery. Does anyone eat celery anymore? I can remember my mother used to have a special dish just for celery. No one these days would be able to figure out what it was for. Had a very distinctive shape, though. Well, it would do, wouldn't it?"

When she had said good-bye to Mrs. Lloyd and tidied up after her, Penny went off in search of Victoria. She found her upstairs, working at the kitchen table, magazines and note-paper spread everywhere.

Victoria looked up and smiled. "Couldn't resist going over some of these spa magazines. The surveyor is going to go over the building this weekend, and if we like what we hear, we should be in a position to make an offer on Monday."

Penny nodded. "That would be good. Well, I'll leave that in your capable hands. By the way," Penny continued, "Mrs. Lloyd has heard that Eirlys is coming to work here and likes the idea so much, she's passing it off as something she dreamed up! Honestly, that woman can be so annoying when we both know the idea was really mine!"

Victoria laughed.

"Excuse me? Whose idea was it? Mine, I think. But yes, Mrs. Lloyd can be very trying at times, but underneath it all she's got a heart of gold and you can't help but like her. Most of the time, anyway. Still, you want to keep on the good side of her because you never know when her local knowledge is going to come in handy. She knows everything there is to know about this town and has done for years. And her memory is still amazingly sharp. She remembers every detail of just about everything that happened."

"That's true."

Penny looked around the kitchen that had once been hers. "You know, it feels strange being here. It's not mine anymore, but I don't feel the cottage is my home yet, either. I feel, well, a little unsettled, really."

"I think you need to lay an old ghost to rest, and then you can move on."

95

"Actually, that's what I came to talk to you about. I'm going to Liverpool on Sunday. The Central Library is open in the afternoon, and I'm going to search through the archives. They'll have copies of the *Echo* dating back decades, and I want to see if there's any mention of Alys."

She started and put her hand over her mouth.

"Oh, I'm so sorry! There's me going on and on and I forgot to ask how you got on when you went to see Bronwyn and Thomas's dog. How was that?"

Victoria stood up and walked over to the sink to fill the kettle. When she returned to the table, she reached into her handbag for her mobile.

"Look, here he is. I took a photo of him."

Penny leaned in to look.

"Oh, he looks adorable in his little basket. I'm sure they're taking really good care of him. What will happen to him, do you think?"

Victoria shot her a wry, knowing look.

Penny grinned.

"Of course they will! They're probably telling themselves all the reasons why they can't keep a dog, but they can say what they like. The outcome's going to be just the same."

She continued to look at the photo.

"You know, I'm not sure I'll ever get used to the idea of looking at photos on a phone. It seems too temporary. I think of them as paper things you hold in your hand. Like the one I found in Emma's pencil box. Like the ones Alwynne has. They're easier to share. I think they're more permanent, too."

She shrugged.

"I know. I'm turning into a fossil. But I like the old ways better. Lots of things just worked better back in the day."

She brightened.

"Anyway, are Thomas and Bronwyn coming over on Friday night? I hope so. There's a lot they can do to help."

"He's coming," replied Victoria. "Bronwyn thinks the dog is too delicate to leave just at the minute."

"Well, fair enough."

"We're going to need stadium seating if our little circle continues to grow," said Victoria as she carried a chair from the dining room into the sitting area. "Who all are you expecting tonight, again?"

"Let's see. Um, well, Alwynne, you and me, of course, and Bethan and Thomas," she said, counting them off on her fingers. "So that's five of us. Gareth isn't coming. Says he's just going to leave us to get on with it."

Victoria set the chair down and wiped off the seat.

"Do I get a sense that things are cooling off a bit there?"

"No, I don't think so. It's just we're both a bit preoccupied with other things right now. You and I have the new business, and then there's this place, and of course the Alys Jones affair. I want to get my wings straight and level before I move on with him. I want everything to be just right. For both of us."

"Well, don't leave it too long is my advice, for what it's worth, or you might find he's moved on without you," said Victoria with an emphatic nod. "He won't wait forever, you know."

Penny looked startled.

"Gosh, I hadn't thought of that. Maybe I'd better find more time for him. How long until they get here? Good, I've got time to make a call. I'll invite him to come with me on Sunday."

As she finished speaking, the doorbell rang, and moments later Alwynne entered.

"Evening, Penny," she said. "Oh, I see you've kept the board up. Good! Well, I've brought another photo to add to it, and I think you're going to like it!"

She reached into a carrier bag and brought out a large brown envelope.

"Here you go," she said as she handed it to Penny, who took it over to the window so she could look at its contents in the early evening light. Alwynne followed her a few moments later and stood silently as Penny withdrew a black-and-white 8 by 10 photo.

The image showed a group of about six teenagers in what looked like an art class. They were grouped around an artfully arranged still-life of fruit, flowers, and a dead bird of some kind, its showy tail feathers trailing mournfully over the edge of the small table.

"Here she is," said Alwynne softly, pointing to a girl in the centre of the group. Penny was surprised that her hand was trembling a little as she handed the photo back to Alwynne.

"Here," she said. "Hold it for a moment while I get my glasses."

A few moments later she examined the photo more closely, her attention focused on the young Alys. She was wearing a school uniform with a crest on the centre of the tunic and a cardigan. She gazed critically at her canvas with a serious look that was difficult to read. Penny couldn't tell if the girl liked what she saw or was dissatisfied with it. Her head was held at a slight incline and her lips were pressed together in what could be critical contemplation of her work. She seemed deeply absorbed in what she was doing, unaware of or uncaring about the camera. Her dark hair was worn in a fringe over her forehead, and the rest of it, all the same length, was cut just under her ears, giving the appearance of a glossy helmet. Penny turned the photo over, noted the date, and did a quick calculation.

"She would have been about fourteen years old here," she murmured.

"Sorry, what did you say?" asked Alwynne, leaning closer.

Penny repeated herself and Alwynne nodded.

"That was taken at the old school. The art teacher's widow donated a lot of his old photos. He was an amateur photographer and enjoyed taking photos of his pupils. Even had a little darkroom at the school and developed the negatives and made the prints himself. Of course, they're both gone now, but it was good of her to pass the photos on to us. You can see how immensely valuable they are. I much prefer the old prints myself to the new digital things that people sometimes e-mail us. Not sure what to do with them. If I save them on a computer, no one will ever see them probably."

After a tactful pause, she added, "So if you do come across any photos in Emma's things that you think have historical merit, you'll be sure to . . ."

Her voice trailed off as Penny nodded and touched her arm.

"Yes, of course I will. You don't have to worry about that. And I agree with you about the photos, by the way. I think it's all about instant gratification versus something of permanent and lasting value, but there are advantages to the digital ones, too, like speed. I haven't turned over Emma's bedroom yet, but I expect there'll be a few treasures there for you. I promised the clothing to Bronwyn for her jumble sale."

"That's the best place for it," agreed Alwynne. "You won't want to wear it, but someone else will. Still, you have a bit of time. The sale isn't until November. Good timing, that, so we can clear out our closets to make room for all the new things we'll get for Christmas."

"You're so practical, aren't you?" said Penny affectionately as the two women smiled at each other.

"Oh, and look—here's the rector. We left the front door open for him."

The Rev. Thomas Evans closed the door behind him and eased into the sitting room with the confidence acquired from many years of attending every imaginable occasion from sickbed visits to the counseling of parents who are beside themselves after learning that their teenage daughter is pregnant.

"Good evening, Penny," he said warmly, reaching over to shake her hand. "And Alwynne, too." He peered around. "Victoria somewhere about, is she?"

From the kitchen came the sound of a ringing telephone, and then a few moments later Victoria joined the group in the living room.

"Hello, Thomas," she said with an easy smile. "That was Bethan on the phone. Says she's sorry she can't make it and that we should carry on."

"Right," said Penny. "That's what we'll do. Why don't we all sit at the dining room table? I think that would work better for us this evening. But first, I want to show Thomas our board and get him up to speed on what we know so far. And, Victoria, there's a new photo here you need to see. It's Alys, when she was about fourteen. She wore her hair quite short. I bet there were a few arguments with her mother over that, but I think she looks quite good."

She handed the photo over to Victoria, who gave it a brief glance, then passed it on to the rector, who carried it with him as he and Penny crossed the room to the whiteboard.

He took a bit more time with it and then returned it to Penny, who taped it to her display.

"I think I'm going to get a small corkboard," she muttered to no one in particular. "I like pushpins better."

She spent a few minutes with the rector, showing him the timeline of the events on the night Alys died and giving as much background as she could. Then, the two joined Victoria and Alwynne at the table.

"Oh dear me," he said as he lowered himself into his chair. "I know you are preoccupied with all this, Penny, but realistically, after all this time, do you think you'll be able to solve a mystery that the police were unable to at the time?"

He paused.

"Well, we did once before," said Penny, referring to the missing bride earlier that summer. "And I, that is we," she said with a vague gesture at the other two, who nodded helpfully, "we need your help. In fact, we need you to do now what you did for us then."

"Oh, no," said the rector. "No more breaking and entering for me. That was quite enough, thank you very much. I am still terrified someone will find out what we did, and I will be up in front of the bishop so fast my feet won't touch the ground."

As the others laughed, he joined in in a good-natured but halfhearted kind of way.

"No," Penny went on, "but you're on the right track. Now, though, we are legally in the cottage so there'll be none of that. However, I hope you'll agree to read Emma's diaries, just as you did last time. But you don't have to read all of them. If you would start in 1967 and go through to 1971."

She gave him her best appealing look. "I can't bear to go through them, and I know you would treat the contents of those journals with the strictest confidence. You are the only person we can trust with this job."

The other two nodded.

"I don't know," he replied uncertainly. "It doesn't seem right to pry into the nature of their relationship, as you described it to me. I don't think I would be comfortable with that."

Penny's mouth turned down at the corners, and an uncomfortable silence hung over the group, broken only by the sound of the rector tapping his fingers on the table.

Don't say anything, Penny thought. Keep quiet just a moment longer and we'll have him.

"Oh well, I guess it won't do any harm," he said at last, giving in with obvious reluctance. "But, mind you, I don't know how soon I might be able to get to them, as we've got our hands rather full at the moment."

He brightened, sat up straighter, and smiled.

"Have you heard about the little dog we found? Of course we're just looking after him temporarily, until a permanent home can be arranged for him, but I must say Bronwyn is enjoying nursing him back to health and she's doing a wonderful job. The little chap gets stronger every day. Won't stay in his basket and follows Bronwyn everywhere. She'll be taking him for walks soon."

The others smiled at him.

"And has he had his follow-up visit to the vet yet?" Victoria asked. "Bronwyn mentioned that something came up and she had to reschedule that."

"That's right, we'll be taking him in next week," the rector replied. "I'm sure Jones, the vet, will be pleased with the dog's progress. Definitely going in the right direction."

Penny cast a sidelong glance at Victoria, acknowledging the deft way she had manipulated the conversation, and then she dived in.

"Well, that's what we were hoping to talk to you about," she began.

"You see, Jones, the vet, is actually the brother of Alys, and we thought that when you take your little dog in to see him . . . by the way, what's the dog's name, again?"

"He doesn't have one. We thought there's no point in us naming him when we aren't going to keep him. We agreed that his proper owners should name him."

Oh, you'll be naming him, all right, thought Penny with an inward smile. That dog isn't going anywhere, except, of course, on another visit to the vet, to be followed soon after by a nice, long walk through the town so his proper new owners can show him off.

"Right, well, when you take the little fellow in to see the vet, I wondered if you or maybe Bronwyn could swing the conversation round to Alys and the accident. I understand from the police reports that Alun was away at university in Edinburgh at the time and the police never interviewed him."

103

"Is there any reason why they should have?" asked the rector.

"I don't really know," said Penny. "That's what we'd like to find out. See if he suddenly goes all shifty, as if he's got something to hide."

The rector laughed.

"Really, Penny! As if he's going to reveal anything about the death of his sister thirty-odd years ago to a couple of clients he barely knows, while he examines a dog in his surgery. And maybe it will cause him some distress, opening up an old wound like that."

Penny looked deflated, and the rector, being a kind soul, responded. "Well, there's no harm in asking, I suppose."

He drained the last of his tea and set the cup down.

"Now, I must be off. I promised Bronwyn I would not be late. Still, I think she enjoys having the occasional evening to herself. Usually spends it curled up with a library book and a glass of sherry, as far as I can tell." He chuckled. "From the covers on them, some of them seem to be quite racy!"

Penny jumped up and ran to the kitchen. She carried the box of Emma's journals that she had saved from the rubbish, through the dining and sitting rooms to the front door, where the rector joined her and opened the door. He went on ahead to open the car door, and she placed the carton on the backseat.

"Now remember," she said, "1967 to 1971. You're looking for references to Alys Jones, and I expect there will be lots of them. We're looking for anything that might shed some light on what happened to Alys. Who their friends were, where they went, any references to a disagreement—anything and everything that you think will help."

104

The rector smiled at her earnest sincerity.

"And thanks so much for doing this. You're the only one we could ask and we do appreciate it."

The rector acknowledged her thanks, got in his car, and with a gentle wave over his shoulder, drove off.

Penny watched as his car made the turn toward town, and then she returned to the cottage.

"I think things will start to move forward now," she said to her friends as she rejoined them at the table. "I'm going to call Gareth and see if he's free on Sunday afternoon. I'm planning a little outing. Not very exciting, I'm afraid, but he might like to come."

She paused for a moment and then continued.

"I'm going to go through the old newspaper microfiche rolls in the library."

Seeing their puzzled looks, she added, "The Central Library. Liverpool. We know how Alys died. We need to know how she lived."

Ten

*P*enny handed her ticket to the conductor and watched as he punched it and then handed it back to her.

"We should be arriving at Chester in about twenty minutes," he said as he turned away to attend to the passenger sitting across the aisle.

"Thank you," Penny murmured to his back, as she tucked the ticket in her handbag.

She shifted in her seat and contemplated the green fields that rolled by the train window. Heavy, grey clouds hung low in the sky, shrouding the tops of the hills. It doesn't look very promising, she thought, glad she had remembered to bring an umbrella. With a small sigh, she picked up the unread *Tatler* that lay forgotten in her lap and stuffed it into her carrier bag.

She tried to think about her plans for the afternoon, but her mind was reluctant to go there. Instead, her last phone conversation with Gareth played out in an endless loop. He had seemed flat and distant at the start of the conversation, and then it got worse. He had declined to come with her to Liverpool.

"I think I'd rather not," he had said. "I don't fancy cooling my heels for four hours while you look through back issues of the *Liverpool Echo*."

What he was really saying, she thought, is "I've got better things to do." It had seemed unnecessarily harsh. And what about the time we could have spent together on the journey there and back? Maybe a nice dinner afterward? A creeping feeling of disquiet and unease alarmed and worried her. She felt she had been taking him emotionally for granted, and now, sensing that he was losing interest in her, she realized how much she didn't want to lose him.

The fields outside the window were gradually giving way to semidetached houses and industrial-type buildings as the countryside was left behind and the landscape changed from rural to urban. The train began to slow and then pulled into the station. She stepped out of the carriage and walked along the platform to the lift that would take her up to the footbridge so she could cross to the other platform to catch the Merseyside train for Liverpool.

She didn't have to wait long and soon found herself in a crowded carriage. Across the aisle four women sat in facing seats with a table between them. In front of each woman was a pile of coins, and with a lot of shouting and hooting, they played cards. At the signal from one, the cards were quickly put away and a carrier bag filled with groceries came out.

Penny watched in amazement as they then silently began to

assemble sandwiches. One woman opened up a tub of margarine and, using a metal knife, spread two slices of white bread. She then handed the bread to the woman beside her, who slapped a piece of grey meat on it and handed it on to the next woman while the first woman spread margarine on two more slices of bread. The third woman placed a piece of sweaty cheese on top of the meat, folded the sandwich together, and handed it to the fourth woman, who added a generous spoonful of coleslaw and then, using the same knife the first woman had used to spread the margarine, cut the sandwich into four and placed the pieces on a paper towel in the centre of the table. No one touched a sandwich until four had been prepared and their little production line shut down. Then, at some unspoken signal, they each grabbed a sandwich and all started talking at once.

How very strange, thought Penny. Wouldn't it be easier to make the sandwiches at home and just wrap them up and bring them along already made? But she had to admit being grateful for the distraction, and by the time the women had eaten their sandwiches and tidied everything away, her journey was over as the train slowed down for the approach into Liverpool Lime Street station.

She got off the train, rode the escalator to the ground floor, and then continued on to the ticket inspection barrier. As she started to fumble in her bag for her ticket, the man guarding the barrier waved her through and she walked to the exit through the seating area and shops of the main concourse.

She paused for a moment to take in the vast iron-and-glass roof, and then, because the main entrance to the station had been closed as part of a massive renovation project, she emerged from a side exit into a day filled with deepening gloom and the heaviness in the air that comes before the relief of rain. Across the way stood the magnificent and recently refurbished St. George's Hall and behind it, on William Brown Street, three great neoclassical buildings, including the Central Library. She worked her way around the side of the Hall, and with an admiring glance at St. John's Garden, picked her way across the cobblestones to the main entrance of the library.

Built in the 1800s, with all the exuberance of the Victorians' passion for grand, intimidating architecture in their public buildings, Liverpool's Central Library is everything a British library should be. Its weathered brown façade, complete with imposing columns, prepares visitors to be impressed.

Penny entered the library and found it surprisingly bright and modern. A helpful attendant at the reception desk pointed her toward the lift, and promising herself more time for browsing on the next visit, she made her way to the fourth floor, where the microfiche copies of the *Liverpool Echo*, along with municipal records, are kept.

After a word with the reference librarian, she was shown the drawers where hundreds of neatly labeled white boxes were stored. Each box contained one month's worth of the newspaper. The librarian pointed out a wooden block, about the same size as one of the white boxes.

"When you remove a box, please put the block in its place so you'll know where to put it back," she requested.

Penny pulled her notebook out of her bag and set it down beside a microfiche reader.

"I'll be just over here if you need any help," said the librarian, who returned to her desk near the entrance.

Having decided she was a start-at-the-beginning kind of

person, Penny pulled the little box that read APRIL 1967 from the drawer and dutifully put the wooden block in its place.

She took the box over to the reader and sat down. She switched on the machine, then removed the spool from the box, threaded it through the magnifier, and wound it forward using the little crank.

She couldn't resist a smile. This seems so low tech, she thought, but when the first page of the *Liverpool Echo* wound into view, she had to admit that low tech as it was, it apparently worked. And you had to admit that storing one month's worth of newspapers in a box just a little bigger than a pack of cigarettes was a huge space saver. But as she turned the little crank that advanced the film forward page by page, she realized the huge drawback. She would have to examine every page looking for one name. Alys Jones. No search and find here. A computer could have pulled the stories she wanted in seconds.

She plowed on through 1967, returning the spool she had finished viewing to its place in the drawer and taking out the next month. Pressed for time because the library closed at four, she tried to resist the temptation to start reading the news stories, but occasionally one caught her eye. The release in June of the *Sgt. Pepper's Lonely Hearts Club Band* LP was big news in the Beatles' hometown. She soon found the advertisements more interesting than the stories. She loved the look of things priced in old money. A man's fine white dress shirt for only five shillings! However much that was.

The years flashed before her. Celebrities died, Pierre Elliott Trudeau was elected prime minister of Canada, the Vietnam War ground on, Martin Luther King, Jr. and Robert Kennedy were assassinated, Richard Nixon was elected president of the United States, the microwave oven was invented, the Concorde made its first flight, and men landed on the moon.

And then, in November 1970, just as she was about to wind on to the next page, she saw a photograph that made her heart beat faster. Taken from an artistic angle, it showed a group of four people laughing as one held up a painting and the three others pretended to judge it.

LIVERPOOL ART TEACHERS PREPARE FOR NEW EXHIBIT
Liverpool artists, left to right, Alys Jones, Millicent Mayhew, and Cynthia Browning sort through canvases in the staff room of the Liverpool School of Art, Hope Street. Looking on is Andrew Peyton, who will be curating the exhibit, scheduled to open in February at the Walker Art Gallery.

She leaned forward to try to get a better look at the grainy black-and-white image. Alys had very short, dark hair and was wearing a tailored white shirt with what looked like a man's tie. She was leaning back in her chair and holding a cigarette in a jaunty but affected kind of way, as if it were in a long cigarette holder.

Penny had to smile. Although she had never been a smoker, she could remember the days when people smoked everywhere—on airplanes, trains, and buses, at meetings and the cinema and even in college and university classrooms, students and professors alike puffing away. That's one thing I definitely don't miss, she thought.

So there was to have been an art exhibit. She wondered if it had gone ahead. The Walker Art Gallery, Penny knew, was

112

next door to the library. She had been there many years before and was now asking herself why she hadn't been back to Liverpool in such a long time. But a visit there would have to wait for another day.

She glanced at her watch. Twenty after three. She reached for her pen to note down the details of the item and then had a better idea. She approached the librarian, who was reading on her computer.

"Excuse me. I'm sorry to trouble you, but I wonder if I could print a page from the microfiche," Penny asked. The librarian's eyes stayed on the screen for a moment, then her head turned in Penny's direction.

"Yes, you may," she said, "but there's a small charge, I'm afraid, and the quality won't be very good."

After carefully placing the copy of the printed page in the file folder in her bag, Penny respooled the film, returned it to its spot, picked out the December spool, and, with slightly shaking fingers, loaded it into the microfiche reader. This one would probably contain the details of Alys's death. In fearful, knowing anticipation of what she was about to see, she wound the reel on slowly. And, sure enough, there it was on the front page of the Monday, December 7, 1970 issue.

LIVERPOOL ARTIST DIES IN HIT-AND-RUN TRAGEDY
A well-liked, promising artist and teacher at the Liverpool School of Art has been killed in a hit-and-run accident.

Alys Jones, 32, died in the early hours of Saturday, December 5 from injuries sustained when she was struck by a car on a back lane in the Welsh market town of Llanelen. Miss Jones, who was born and grew up in Llanelen, was believed to have been visiting family at the time of the accident.

The driver has not been caught, and police are asking anyone who might have information to come forward. The investigation continues.

Friends and colleagues at the college are devastated by Miss Jones's death.

Close friend and fellow artist Millicent Mayhew said, "We are reeling from the loss. Not only have we lost a dear and treasured friend but the Liverpool art movement has lost a great talent. She was among the best painters of her generation and will be missed by all who knew her."

Miss Jones had been due to exhibit her work, along with that of other artists from the Liverpool School of Art, at the Walker Art Gallery in February.

Funeral arrangements have not been announced.

Penny sent the page to the printer and, realizing that the librarian was waiting to close for the day, spooled the film back to the beginning of the reel, put it back in the box, and replaced it in the drawer. She gathered up her bags and, nodding a thank you to the librarian, who was switching off her computer, left the room and descended the stairs to the main exit.

She found herself on the street and, a few steps later, outside the Walker Gallery, now closed. She took in the colourful banners promoting the current exhibits and promised herself she would return soon and give herself more time. A visit to the art gallery would be a must.

114

The journey home seemed to go very quickly, and Penny had changed trains at Chester before she knew it. Lost in thought, she went over the few details she had learned and wondered how she could find this Millicent Mayhew woman, if she was still alive.

Perhaps someone at the old Liverpool School of Art, now part of John Moores University, could help. She'd try to make some calls tomorrow. And then she remembered that Eirlys, her new assistant, was starting the next day. She'd have to spend the day training her, but once that was done, she should have more free time to pursue other things.

And, she realized, she hadn't been painting in ages. She resolved to contact Alwynne and get the sketching club together for an outing. Thinking that her to-do list was getting longer by the minute, she put her head back on the seat, closed her eyes, and lulled by the rhythm of the train, fell asleep. When she awoke, the train was just pulling in to Llandudno Junction. She sighed, picked up her bag, and prepared for the arrival in Llandudno and the short walk to catch the bus to Llanelen.

And then she remembered Gareth and realized she hadn't thought about him for hours.

She arrived home tired and hungry but reasonably happy with her day's work. Not only had she discovered a couple of possible leads into Alys's last days and the people who knew her, but she felt invigorated by the visit to Liverpool. She vowed to go again, and soon. Maybe Victoria could come with her. Being a day-tripper was all right, but an overnight stay would be more fun and they could get in some good shopping. Perhaps they could stop in a rather nice hotel in the centre of the city. The getaway would have to be with Victoria, as Gareth hadn't seemed interested and the hotel business with him might be a bit tricky. Or would it? Maybe that would be the best route to go.

After popping a frozen chicken korma in the oven and retrieving the items she had printed from the *Liverpool Echo,* she taped the photo to the whiteboard and then stood back, arms folded, contemplating it. She remained lost and absorbed in the image until the ringing of the telephone startled her back to reality. Hoping it would be Gareth, she answered it on the fourth ring.

"Hello? Oh, Thomas, yes, good evening. Fine, thanks."

A few minutes later she thanked him, replaced the receiver, sank into the comfort of the sofa, and stared unseeing at the photos on the whiteboard.

Four of Emma's diaries were missing. Yes, he was sure. He'd checked and double-checked. The years 1967 to 1970 were not there. And 1971 contained nothing of interest.

Eleven

"Well, that tells us something, then, doesn't it?" said Victoria on Monday morning as they prepared to open the salon. "Someone who didn't want us to find out the truth must have got in somehow and removed those books from the cottage. It goes to show that there's something very wrong here. I think it confirms our suspicions that Alys's death was no accident."

"Hmm," said Penny. "Maybe. Or maybe not. Maybe Emma got rid of them herself."

"Could be," agreed Victoria. "But why would she do that?" She thought for a moment. "I don't think she would. I think it's more likely to be the other way round—she'd get rid of all the others and keep just the ones that covered the Alys years." The sound of knocking on the salon door ended the discussion.

"Anyway, we'll have to leave it at that for now," she said as she stood up to open the door. "That'll be Eirlys, right on time, ready for her first day at work. Are you free for dinner? Let's get together later and I can fill you in on my meeting today at the new site with the surveyors." She looked back over her shoulder at Penny, who nodded.

A moment later, ponytail bobbing and sporting a bright smile, Eirlys bounded confidently into the salon clutching a large brown envelope.

"I wanted to show you my certificate," she said to Penny. "See, it shows I passed the course and am qualified now to do the manicures!"

"Well, that's wonderful, Eirlys." Penny smiled. "Let's put you to work, shall we? I thought we'd start with a little bit of orientation to the shop so you can get to know where everything is." She pointed to the appointments book. "Let's start here. Our first client should be here in about twenty minutes, so we need to make sure everything's ready for her. You'll find that we leave the shop tidy before we close for the night so everything is pretty much ready to go when we open in the morning. That'll be your last job of the day. Still, there are always a few last-minute things to do in the morning.

"And your first task can be to put the kettle on. Mine's a coffee with a little bit of extra milk and a sweetener, and you can ask Victoria if she wants one. You won't mind brewing up for us and the clients, will you? And yourself, too, of course! You'll find everything in the little pantry just beside the supply cupboard. Oh, the supply cupboard! Well, we'll get to that later."

Penny smiled to herself as Eirlys bustled off on her first task. If Eirlys did as well as she thought she would, Penny was glad to give her the work, and as soon as Eirlys was able to take on more responsibility, she'd have more time for what she really wanted to do. Victoria's time, of course, would soon be totally taken up managing the renovations for the new spa building, and she would be spending very little time in the salon. After a quick welcoming word with Eirlys, Victoria had already left on the short walk to the site to meet with the surveyor who would be doing the building inspection.

Penny had wanted to discuss the Gareth situation with Victoria, but there'd been no time this morning, and after the call from Thomas last night, she'd had other things to think about.

Penny planned to show Eirlys the ropes and then, if she was doing well, leave her for an hour or so while she went upstairs and made a few phone calls.

The September morning was just about perfect. A few wisps of fluffy clouds swept across a bright blue sky. A gentle breeze played with the hem of Victoria's scarf as she walked across the cobbled town square on her way to the riverfront building that she and Penny hoped would soon become their new spa. Both felt somewhat apprehensive at the amount of money the conversion would cost, but they were confident that the numbers in their business plan would hold. Of course, one couldn't plan for a recession or other economic downturns, but all things considered, with the recent revival of tourism to North Wales and the increased demand for spa treatments, they believed in their future.

As she passed the Red Dragon Hotel, Victoria considered popping in for a moment to say hello to Mrs. Geraint, the day desk clerk. In a few weeks Victoria could well be approaching the hotel manager to ask if he would consider partnering with them to provide light meals and overnight accommodations for the spa's out-of-town guests. She thought he would probably leap at the chance, and now might be a good time to begin softening them up because she and Penny would also want the hotel to refurbish guest rooms for spa clients.

But she decided to leave that for another day and kept going. She was almost past the entrance to the hotel when she noticed a familiar figure emerging from the front door. It was Gareth and he was not alone. A smiling woman walked confidently beside him. They were not touching, but there was a certain knowing intimacy in the way she was looking up at him that made Victoria's stomach clench. She quickened her pace and, ducking into the nearest building, found herself in the local organization that promoted the Welsh language. She picked up a brochure and peeked out the window. The pair walked toward the street, and Gareth helped the woman into her car. He then set off in the direction of the Red Dragon car park, presumably to find his own vehicle.

Victoria gave the young man who ran the operation a weak smile.

"Are you interested in taking Welsh lessons, then?" he asked pleasantly. "We hold them every week in the community centre, and I'm sure there would be a time that would suit you. We do afternoon and evening classes. It's not as difficult as you might think," he added helpfully.

Thinking of the endless string of strange consonant combinations and the difficulty she had in pronouncing even the simplest of Welsh words, Victoria declined.

"I'm not very good at picking up languages, I'm afraid. Perhaps in the future," she said, "but not just at the moment, thank you."

"Well, feel free to keep the brochure," said the young man, with a small gesture at the brochure in her hand. "And, of course, we'll be here if you change your mind. Good-bye." And then, for good measure, he said it in Welsh, "*Da boch*," and gave her an encouraging nod.

"*Da boch*," Victoria dutifully replied and left the premises. A minute later she realized she was still holding the brochure with its beautiful cover art featuring a panoramic view of the brilliant green Conwy Valley.

She tried to push the image of Gareth with the woman to the edge of her mind so she could focus on the meeting with the surveyor. The question, of course, was should she tell Penny she'd seen him. Well, she'd think about that over the course of the day. Arriving at the riverfront property, she opened her briefcase, pulled out a notebook, and tucked the Welsh language brochure inside. The building inspector, wearing a high-visibility bright yellow vest with orange stripes and a blue hard hat, was gazing up at the roof with a worried look on his face and a clipboard cradled in his arms.

"Well, should we have good news or bad news first?" asked Penny. They were seated at her dining room table, take-away Thai cartons spread out before them.

"Let's have the good news," said Victoria as she passed the spring rolls to Penny.

"Eirlys was absolutely wonderful! Really capable and so

cheerful to have around. I can ask her to do anything and she's happy to do it. It won't be long before I can leave her to it. I left her alone in the shop for an hour while I made telephone calls and she just carried right on, seeing to everything. Has really good instincts and judgment, I'd say. Knows how to put the customers at ease. So that's a positive. What about you?"

Victoria took another bite of pad thai and put down her chopsticks.

"The building's about what we expected it to be, but the roof and guttering will need to be replaced. Still, apparently there's no major cracking or movement or structural weakness. Based on his preliminary findings, the surveyor says he can recommend that we go ahead and make an offer—but to allow at least thirty thousand for the roof repairs. Oh, and there's something wrong with the duct work. A blockage of some sort. Could be anything . . . old rats' nest, maybe. But that'll need sorting."

"Well, that's good news, surely?" said Penny. "You don't look very cheery about it. I feel a 'but' coming. *Is* there a 'but' coming?"

Victoria shook her head and was unable to look Penny in the eye. She picked up her wineglass and inspected its contents.

"What is it?" prompted Penny. "You've got me really worried now. Has something happened?"

Victoria set down her wineglass and sighed.

"Look," she said, "I don't want to upset you, and I wasn't even sure if I should mention it, but I know what you're like and I think you'd want to know."

Penny's eyes widened and she leaned forward.

"What? Tell me. Whatever it is, just tell me. Please."

"Um, well, it's just that I saw Gareth coming out of the Red Dragon this morning and, ah, I'm afraid he wasn't alone."

In the heavy, awkward silence Penny set down her fork, slumped forward, and looked at the table, resting her hands on her queasy stomach.

"That explains Sunday, I guess," she said finally. "I'd asked him if he wanted to come to Liverpool with me and he said no, he didn't fancy it. I thought there was something awkward about it—a distance, a chilliness—and I guess I know why now."

She raised her shoulders in a protective, dismissive shrug.

"That's that, then, I guess."

She dipped and twirled a spring roll in its sauce, took a bite, and then set the rest down.

"You know, I'm suddenly not very hungry," she said, picking up her napkin and wiping her mouth. "I'm going to put the kettle on. Be back in a few minutes."

Victoria waited. Some time passed before she heard the sound of water running and the kettle filling. Penny returned, wearing a weak, apologetic smile and wreathed in disappointment. Her eyes were red and puffy and she was clutching a tissue. She glanced at it, then stuffed it in her pocket before she sat down.

"Right, then. Let me tell you what I've learned about Alys."

Victoria smiled and made an encouraging "the floor is yours" kind of sweeping gesture.

"When she died," Penny began, "Alys and two other artists were getting ready for an art exhibit. She was still young, early thirties, so this would likely have been her first major showing *and* it was to be held at the Walker Gallery, which would have been a big deal. It very likely would have launched her. I don't know if the exhibit went ahead or not after her death, but I need to find that out."

She paused for a moment to jot down a couple of sentences in her notebook and then looked at Victoria.

"It's hard, isn't it, to know what's important and what isn't? Does it matter whether the exhibit was held or not? I don't know."

"Neither do I. But go on."

"Right. Where was I? Oh yes, the exhibition. Also showing their work were Millicent Mayhew and Cynthia Browning. I found a photo of them in the *Echo* and printed it off. It's over there now on the board." She gestured with her head in the direction of the sitting room. "Cynthia had big blond hair, and Millicent looked quite plain and ordinary. And then there was Andrew Peyton, who was the curator."

"What's a curator do, exactly?"

"He's the person responsible for organizing the exhibit. He decides what pieces will be shown and in what order. He also determines the point of view or theme of the whole thing."

"Doesn't sound like that would take very long."

"They can also be responsible for acquisitions and preservation of collections, so the job can be a bit broader. Anyway, this Andrew Peyton was the curator. So we need to find out about these three. We need to know if they're still alive, where they are now, and if we can talk to them. I rang the art school today—it's part of the university now—but the woman I talked to hadn't heard of any of them."

"So you had a good day at the library, though?"

124

"It wasn't wasted, that's for sure. But something struck me as I was leaving. The librarian switched off her computer."

Victoria snorted. "Well, she would do, wouldn't she? What about it?"

"It made me think back to the old days when women had typewriters, and at the end of the day there would be this little ritual about shaking out the plastic cover and placing it over the typewriter. That would be the signal that you were finished and going home."

"And in the morning, she'd come into the office and pull the cover off the typewriter, and that would be the start of the day, I suppose."

"Yeah."

"So?"

"I don't know. I was just thinking about it, that's all."

"I'd be careful if I were you. You're starting to sound really old."

Penny laughed. "Am I? I guess I am. Anyway, what do I care? I've never even had a job where I had to use a typewriter. Can barely remember them, as a matter of fact. There was one in the background of that photo, though, and I guess that's what made me think about this."

She thought for a moment.

"Alwynne was saying something like that . . . sometimes the value in old photos is in the background details. Things like what people were wearing or what's on the table."

She shrugged and then began to twirl her pencil. She did not look at Victoria.

"What was she like, this woman you saw with Gareth? Was she young? Attractive?"

125

"Not as attractive as you, that's for sure. Nothing special. In her late forties, maybe. I didn't have that much time to look at her. But remember, Penny, things aren't always what they seem. There may be a perfectly innocent explanation. You should be careful not to jump to conclusions."

"Right!" said Penny. "Like she'd be his sister visiting from Cardiff, maybe."

"Oh, does he have a sister in Cardiff? I didn't know."

A ghost of a smile crossed the corners of Penny's mouth. "Oh, Victoria, I don't know if he has a sister in Cardiff. I was just saying that as an example."

"Oh, right."

"Maybe it was the sex thing. I think he wanted to, and I wasn't ready, so I guess he found himself someone who was up for it."

"Oh, so you two haven't actually . . ."

She blushed.

"Sorry! None of my business."

Penny shook her head.

"It wasn't that I didn't want to, I do, I mean I did. But I'm a lot older now and my body isn't what it used to be. Doesn't look the way it used to. There are things I'm self-conscious about. That doesn't seem to matter as much for men, but, well, you know."

Victoria nodded. "Yeah, I know what you mean. I don't think it matters too much if you've been with the same old guy for years and the two of you are comfortable together, but with someone new and for the first time, at our age, yes, I can see exactly how you'd feel."

"And not only that, but there's the business of where. I

wanted it to be nice for us. Romantic, even. Not his place where he used to live with his wife—not that I've ever been there; it might be quite nice for all I know—and not here, not yet, not with all these memories of Alys and Emma and their stuff everywhere you look. I wanted to wait until the place was all done up nicely and looking the way I want it to. I'd even thought, maybe a hotel, and then you see him and that's exactly where he is. So he and I were thinking along the same lines, only it just wasn't me he wanted, apparently."

Her eyes began to swim and she reached in her pocket for a tissue as Victoria crept into the living room and returned with a box of them.

"Here. Treat yourself. Have a new one."

After a moment Victoria put her elbow on the table and rested her chin on her hand. "What will you do if he rings? Will you see him?"

"The way I feel now, I think I'd be too embarrassed. How could I?"

"Maybe you should give him the chance to explain."

"I don't think so."

And then she started to gather up the remains of the meal, indicating that as far as she was concerned, the subject was closed.

"I'll give you a hand," said Victoria as she picked up the cutlery, and together they cleared the table.

"Do you want me to stay and help with the dishes?" she asked when the leftovers had been scraped into plastic containers and stored in the fridge.

"No thanks," said Penny. "I'm going to watch a bit of telly and then an early night. But there is something you can do, if you don't mind. Please call Alwynne and Thomas and Bronwyn and see if they can come over on Friday night. I want to hear about the visit to the vet. I hope they learned something that will help us."

"And what about Bethan?" asked Victoria. "Or is she out of the picture now, too?"

"Hmm. We need her, and anyway, we like her, so if we can, let's keep in with her."

They stood there awkwardly for a few moments, and then Victoria turned toward the door.

"Well. Good night, then."

"Good night. And hey, thanks for telling me. What was that expression I read once and liked so much? Oh yes, 'the uglier the truth, the truer the friend who tells you.'"

"It's just amazing the difference in him," Rev. Thomas Evans was saying to his wife, Bronwyn. "Look at him sitting there looking at you."

The difference in the dog was remarkable. His beige coat had been brushed, his body was filling out, and his eyes had become bright and joyful. He walked easily on his lead, gobbled up every morsel in his bowl, and once he was strong enough to go outside, barked at the door to be let out. He played in the rectory garden but, Bronwyn noticed, never strayed into the cemetery. The first few nights she had placed his basket beside her bed and now, without being asked, as soon as he saw them begin their bedtime routine he had his own. While Thomas checked to make sure the door was locked, the dog had a final drink of water. When Bronwyn turned off the lights in the sitting room, he waited at the bottom of the stairs. As the couple headed toward the stairs, he bounded up ahead of them and greeted them at the top. Then he scampered down the hall and led them to their bedroom.

"Well, he's getting along splendidly," Alun Jones said the next morning. "He's gaining weight and looking much better in himself. How have you been finding him?"

"Oh, he's the best little dog anyone could ask for!" Bronwyn replied. "So eager to please and such a dear, good boy."

The vet and the rector exchanged a quick glance.

"Well, I'm going to suggest that he stay with you a few more days, just to be on the safe side, and then, if you're sure you wouldn't be able to keep him yourself, we'll see about finding him a forever home."

The couple looked at each other.

"Yes, that would be best," said Thomas. "It's the time, you see. All that walking."

"Of course," agreed the vet. "But while he's here, we'll just make sure his immunizations are up to date. If you could hold him just there, I'll get these into him."

Bronwyn cleared her throat.

"I'm sure this is going to sound very strange," she began, after an anxious glance at her husband, "but I wondered about your sister, Alys, who died all those years ago."

Jones looked shocked, and then a wave of quiet sadness washed over his face.

"Alys?" he said uncertainly, as he began to fill two syringes. The name sounded frozen in time, as if he hadn't said it in years.

"Yes, um, I was wondering, that is, a friend of ours has recently inherited some property that seems to have a connection to Alys, and we, that is, Thomas and I, were wondering if you remembered anything unusual that happened around the time she died. Our friend, you see, is curious about it."

Jones said nothing and the silence was deafening.

"Oh, I am so sorry," said Bronwyn. "I shouldn't have mentioned it."

"No, you're all right," said Jones, looking at the rector, who looked uncomfortable but very interested at the same time. "It's just that I hadn't thought about all that in a long time. I was away at school in Scotland when it happened, and she was a good few years older than me, so I wasn't that involved in her life. I came home for the funeral, of course. My parents, especially my mother, were devastated. In some ways, I don't think she ever got over it. There was one thing that really upset her, though, that she did think strange, and that was that Alys left so little work behind. My mother would have loved to have had more of her paintings, but there was just the one, as far as I know, and my brother has it now.

"I know my mother always wondered about that. To be honest, she also didn't think the police did as much as they could have to find out who did it."

He rubbed the dog's fur where he'd given him the injections.

"Now, about our little friend here. Would you like me to ask around to find a new owner for him? We won't have any trouble finding a home for him."

Thomas lifted the dog down.

"Yes, that might be best," Thomas said.

Bronwyn's face tightened as she bent over to clip the lead on the dog's collar.

"And this friend of yours who wants to know the details of my sister's death," Jones said. "May I ask who that is?"

"It's Penny Brannigan, the manicurist. She recently inherited Emma Teasdale's cottage."

They thanked the vet and led the dog from the surgery. Jones folded his arms and watched them go, knowing that no one else would be getting this little dog anytime soon. As he turned to enter notes on the computer, a dark look of grief and anxiety passed across his face as an unfamiliar emotion surged through him.

And then he ripped a page off a prescription pad, wrote Penny's name on it, and slipped the paper into his pocket.

When the Evanses returned home, Bronwyn lifted the little dog out of the car and smiled as he scampered up the path to the kitchen door.

"His tail never stops wagging, does it?" she commented as Thomas put the key in the door. "I'll put the kettle on, and then we're going to have a little chat, you and I."

"Of course, my dear," said Thomas as he hung his jacket on the back of a chair, then pulled it out and sat on it.

Bronwyn filled the kettle, set it on the stove, and then joined him.

"Thomas," she began. "I've been thinking."

"Have you, dear? What about?"

"About you. And your health. We both know it would be very good for both of us if we were to take more exercise. Perhaps you could do more walking on your parish visits."

Thomas cocked his head and smiled at her. "Go on."

"Yes, and if you were to have a little companion to take with you, I'm sure that would cheer up some of your elderly shut-ins."

"A little companion, such as . . .," said Thomas, with a warm glint in his eye.

"Oh! You know what I'm saying! I'm saying that this dear little dog belongs right here with us. We've become that fond of him and he of us, we can't give him up now. I've worked it out and we can easily manage his food out of the housekeeping, and he won't be any trouble at all."

"Come here, darling," said Thomas, pulling her onto his lap. "Of course, he's staying with us. I was going to ask you today if it would be all right with you! Now, we need to have a name for him. Do you have any thoughts?"

"Let me think. Do you have any ideas?"

"Well, there is one," said the rector. "In fact, I had this made up for him in Llandudno when I was there a few days ago. I hope you'll agree to it."

He reached into his pocket and pulled out a dog tag in the shape of a bone. On one side was a little Welsh red dragon and on the other a boy's name.

"Oh, it's perfect! I love it!" said Bronwyn.

"Robbie."

"Woof!"

The sound of laughter filled the bright, sunny kitchen.

Twelve

*A*re you coming with me to Penny's this evening, dear?" the rector asked his wife over a supper of cold roast beef and salad on Friday evening. "I'd like to," Bronwyn replied and then, glancing down at Robbie sitting patiently beside her chair, added, "Do you think she'd mind if I bring Robbie? I don't feel right to leave him."

"I'll just give her a quick ring and ask, but I'm sure she'll be fine with it. Penny loves dogs. I'll ring her right after dinner. This salad is delicious, by the way."

"That'll be the new Asian sesame dressing. We've not had it before." She laughed. "Oh, look at us! Keeping a dog and eating fancy foreign food. What are we like?"

·   ·   ·

The Evanses, with Robbie in Bronwyn's arms, were the last to arrive at Penny's. She greeted them warmly, making a great fuss over the dog.

"So this is the little chap I've been hearing so much about," she said as she fondled a silky ear. "Well, bring him in. I've put down a bowl of water for him in the kitchen, and here's a little pup-warming present for you."

She gave Bronwyn a box of gourmet dog biscuits tied in a bright red bow with little Dalmatians on it. Then she gestured toward the sitting area.

Alwynne, who was seated in a wing chair near the archway to the dining room, rose to greet them.

Penny joined the group and, after making sure everyone had a drink, invited them to sit down. Bronwyn scooped up Robbie, who had been wandering around giving everything a good sniff. He promptly curled up on her lap and, after one last look around the room, closed his eyes and went to sleep as Penny took her place in front of the group.

"I'd like to start by filling you in on what I've learned this week," she began, "and adding to that a very important piece of information that Bronwyn and the rector, here"—she nodded and smiled in their direction—"have given us.

"At the time of her death Alys had been getting ready to participate in an art showing along with two other artists." She consulted her notebook. "Millicent Mayhew and Cynthia Browning they were called. The curator of the show was an Andrew Peyton, and the four were photographed together just a month before Alys died. The show was to have been held in February 1971 and Alys was killed in December."

She wrote the three names on the board and then continued.

"Now, Bronwyn and Thomas learned from Jones, the vet, Alys's brother, that his parents were surprised that she had left so few paintings behind. But that doesn't make any sense, does it?" She looked from one to the other.

"Of course it doesn't! If she had a show coming up in two months, there should have been lots of paintings. But, so far, we only know about two. This one"—she pointed at the painting of the couple on the picnic that she had hung near the display board—"that belonged to Emma and its companion painting that now hangs in Richard Jones's office. And that painting, according to Alun Jones, had been in the possession of his family."

The rector nodded.

"So the question is this: What happened to the rest of her paintings?"

No one spoke.

"Well, there are a couple of things for us to consider. For every major artist, their work becomes more valuable after their death. That's easy to understand. The creation of the work is over. There won't be any more. Supply and demand. So someone who had access to the paintings might have killed her, and then hoped the publicity around her death would drive the value of the work up. That person might have hidden the paintings somewhere, and when the time is right, they'll be 'discovered.' However, the problem with that theory is that if they do surface, the paintings are obviously the property of the Jones brothers, so it's difficult to see how someone else could profit from that scenario.

"So I think something happened to them, but I don't know what, yet. But I think the missing paintings are telling us that

135

Alys's death was no accident. I think she was murdered, and whoever killed her has the paintings. Or had them."

The rector cleared his throat and looked at his hands, Bronwyn continued to stroke the sleeping Robbie on her lap, and Alywnne looked at Victoria, who looked at Penny.

The silence hung heavily over them as each pondered what Penny had said.

"I called the art college this week to see if anyone there knew anything about these three characters—Millicent, Cynthia, and Andrew—but the young woman I spoke to had never heard of them, didn't have a clue what I was talking about, and to be honest, I don't think she cared very much. Why should she? Long before her time."

Penny's shoulders sagged and she ran her fingers desperately through her hair, leaving one side standing up wildly.

"So I'm wondering if anyone has any suggestions on what our next steps should be. We've got to find out more about these three."

Victoria got up from her chair, took a biscuit off the table, and returned to her place. She took a bite and then delicately picked a few crumbs off her skirt.

"Well, what about this then?" suggested the rector. "Everybody writes down the names of these three people we're looking for, and we'll all go home and put on our thinking caps. If anyone comes up with something, ring Penny or bring it to the meeting next week."

He peered at her. "There will be a meeting next week, won't there?"

He smiled at everyone, then nodded encouragingly.

"Well, then," he said to Bronwyn, "if there's nothing else, shall we be on our way?"

Bronwyn set Robbie on the floor, clipped on his lead, and after saying their good-byes, they made their way to the front door, where Alwynne and Penny joined them. Penny walked with them down the short path that led to the street. The outside light shone on Robbie's blond fur, and Penny smiled at the sight of his sturdy back legs and wagging tail as he set off to lead the little party safely home.

She waved good-bye, then turned and walked back to the cottage, stepped inside, closed the door behind her, and leaned on it. Victoria walked toward her across the sitting room.

"Gareth just rang. I said you were out—well, you were, sort of. Said I didn't think you'd be very long. And you weren't."

Penny winced.

"Sorry! But really, Penny, I think you owe it to him to talk to him. He sounded rather low."

"Well good. Serves him right. I've been feeling a bit down myself over the last few days, in case you hadn't noticed," Penny replied.

"Look, I'd hoped we could get caught up on the building tonight, but I think I'm going to go now. I'll see you tomorrow and we can talk then. How are you getting on with Eirlys, by the way? The clients really seem to like her. We're almost fully booked, and we'll soon have to set up another table."

"She is wonderful!" Penny agreed. "You should have seen her charming Mrs. Lloyd this week. Mrs. Lloyd wanted me to do her nails but kept glancing over at Eirlys. I think she'll be asking for her in a week or two. I'm so glad I thought of getting Eirlys in."

"Yes, very clever of you." Victoria grinned. "Anyway, Gareth said he'd ring back, so I'm going to leave you to it. Whatever you decide to do, I'm sure it'll be for the best. At least at our age we know how to deal with these situations."

Penny's eyes clouded. "What would you do if you were me?"

"I'd listen to what he has to say. I think he's a genuine, sincere man who cares about you. I think you're afraid of being hurt and of being vulnerable. But you already are involved, anyway, so it's too late."

She gave an apologetic shrug. "God, I almost wish I'd never mentioned it now. But, Penny, do hear him out. He'll probably have some big reason. Men always do."

Sensing something but not knowing what, she touched Penny on the arm. "What is it?"

Penny shrugged and looked away. "I'm not sure I'd know what to say. I don't think I'd feel comfortable with that conversation. I think I'd rather just let it go."

Victoria peered at her. "Well, maybe when the time feels right." She glanced at her watch. "I'm off. See you tomorrow."

Penny returned to the living room and stared at the names she had written on the whiteboard: Andrew Peyton, Millicent Mayhew, Cynthia . . . at the sound of her ringing telephone, half expected but nevertheless startling in the stillness, she stopped and turned to look at the phone. She let it ring until it went to voice mail. She looked at the phone for a few more seconds, then returned to her whiteboard and started writing down questions:

Where is Alys's artwork now?

Did she have any enemies?

Penny thought for a moment and then added the word *fren-emies?* Thinking it was an awful word with even worse implications, she considered the idea that people are usually killed by someone they knew and often that person was a wolf in sheep's clothing—an enemy disguised as a friend. Someone the victim knew and trusted.

She set the marker down on the whiteboard ledge, then sat down on the sofa that faced it.

And who would Alys have known best and trusted the most? In her personal life, it would have been Emma. In her professional life, it probably was Andrew Peyton, who was preparing the exhibit that would have launched her career.

Penny got up off the sofa and returned to the whiteboard. Picking up the marker, she added to the list:

Did the exhibit go ahead?

The answer to that, she decided, would tell her a lot. She reached for her notebook and made a note to call the Walker Gallery. She doubted anyone would be available on Saturday, and the answer would probably have to wait until next week. But in the meantime, the Llanelen library would be open tomorrow, and she could use the computer there to see what she could find out about the Liverpool three.

The next morning, Penny arrived at the salon almost half an hour before opening time to sort out a box of new samples, and soon after, Eirlys knocked on the door.

"Blimey, Eirlys," said Penny as she let her in, "you're early this morning."

"Morning, Penny," Eirlys replied brightly. "I was hoping you'd be here. I wanted to ask you something. There's a fall dance coming up at the school, and I wondered what you would think of the idea of offering a student rate. I know lots of the girls would love to come in for a manicure. Most of them have never even had one, so this would be a good way to introduce them to the idea of coming to the salon, even if just for special occasions."

"That's a great idea, Eirlys, and I'll discuss it with Victoria and we'll think about it. The problem is that if we offer a student rate, we'll also have to offer a seniors' rate, and I just don't know if we can swing that right now. But it's definitely something to consider, and I want you to bring all your ideas to me.

"Now, let's have a look at who's coming in this morning. I'd like to leave you in charge here while I slip out for a bit."

"If you're going to the library to use the computer, why don't you just buy one?" Eirlys asked innocently as she filled a glass container with cotton balls.

"I want to," Penny replied, "but I don't know that much about them. I don't know what kind to get."

"You should talk to my brother, then. He'll help you, and he knows everything there is to know about computers."

"Of course he does." Penny smiled. "That's why you young people are so great to have around."

She handed Eirlys a small stack of towels and glanced at her watch.

"Anyway, Mrs. Morgan should be here in about ten minutes, so I'm going to leave you to it. I'll be back at lunchtime to take over, so I'll see you then."

Eirlys folded a towel exactly as Penny had shown her, neatly into thirds with the seams and label to the inside, and added it to the stack on the shelf above the sink.

"How about this, then, Penny? We offer the students a discounted rate, say one pound off, just for the dance? There'll be a set time limit. One week only! I'll get my brother to make up a nice sign on his computer, and we'll post it in the window." She paused for a moment and then added eagerly, "And I'll be the one to do the girls' nails; you don't have to worry about that."

Penny laughed. "I admire your enterprise, Eirlys! All right, then, go on. We'll start with that. One week only!"

"And then . . ." Eiryls glanced at Penny as if seeking approval to continue. "Well, it's just that you mentioned the senior ladies would want something, too, so I thought perhaps in the run up to Christmas, you might offer the pensioners a one-pound-off special deal, too."

"Hmm. I like it," agreed Penny. "Or maybe in the week between Christmas and New Year's, when things are a bit slow."

Penny gave Eirlys a little pat on the arm and then left the shop, headed up Station Road in the direction of the library.

"Hello." She smiled at Rhian, seated behind her desk.

"Computer?" she asked. Penny nodded.

"Right. I'll put you on number eight and give you an hour, as we're not too busy."

Penny thanked her and settled in front of the computer.

141

She took out her notebook, called up Google, and went to work.

The time flew by and a very fast hour later, she closed her notebook and signed off the computer.

"That was really helpful," she said to Rhian on the way out. "Thanks very much. I was thinking about getting myself a coffee. May I get you one?"

"How kind! No coffee, for me, thanks, that's part of my problem. But I'm all alone here for the next two hours, and if you'd just wait there for a moment, in case someone comes, I'd love to pop along to the loo. Would you mind?"

"No, I'd be glad to."

Penny stood in front of the counter while the librarian pulled her handbag out of the desk drawer and disappeared through a door marked PRIVATE.

A few minutes later she returned, and Penny left the library. She hurried along the street back to the salon and poked her head in the door. Eirlys was concentrating on her work, but the client looked over and, when she saw who it was, smiled.

"Hello!" said Penny. "Everything all right?"

"Just grand, thanks. Your new assistant is doing a wonderful job."

"Good! Glad to hear it. Eirlys, have you seen Victoria? Is she here or at the site, do you know?"

"She's upstairs in her flat, working on some papers."

"Right. I'll just pop up and see her then, and I'll be back in about half an hour and you can take your lunch break."

She closed the door and walked a few steps to the edge of the building and scampered up the circular wrought-iron stairs that led to the small flat above the salon that had once been hers; when she moved into Emma's cottage, Victoria had taken it over. She knocked on the glass door and waited for Victoria to answer it.

A few minutes later Victoria tugged open the door.

"You gave me a real fright. No one uses that door, and you should know by now that you don't have to knock. What were you thinking?"

"Sorry! I just thought it would be better to come this way than through the salon. I've got so much to tell you. You won't believe what I've found out."

"Well, you'd better come in, then. Do you want anything to drink? Tea? Biscuit?"

"No, thanks. I'm bursting to tell you what I learned at the library on the Internet this morning." She flipped open her notebook.

"Right. Let's start with Cynthia Browning. She's supposed to have emigrated to New Zealand. Anyway, she seems to have been a pretty minor player in the Liverpool art scene."

Penny looked up from her notebook.

"But Millicent did better for herself. She had a couple of successful shows and got fairly good reviews. 'Work shows great promise' sort of thing. But then she got arthritis and had to give up her painting career. Still, her paintings sell reasonably well today. She's considered almost, but not quite, in the same league as Stuart Sutcliffe."

She closed the notebook with a flourish.

"And . . ." Victoria prompted.

"And what?"

"And what about the man? The curator?"

"Ah. I couldn't find anything about him. But . . . and here's the best bit . . . there's a multimedia exhibit opening at the Victoria Gallery and Museum in Liverpool in a couple of weeks that's going to be perfect for us. It's a retrospective of Liverpool artists from the 1960s, featuring Stuart Sutcliffe and his contemporaries. It's got photographs by Edward Chambré Hardman, poetry, art, everything from the period. Can't wait! Will you come with me?"

"Maybe. I'll think about it."

"What if I told you there'll be paintings by Millicent Mayhew?"

"Now I'm interested. Let me know what day."

"Right. I'd better get back downstairs now so Eirlys can go on her break."

"Good. And I hope that means you're really going to get back to work. I'm starting to wonder how you ever managed without her. And don't forget we've got an appointment on Monday with Jones, the solicitor, to sign the papers on the new spa."

"Good morning, ladies. Right on time, I see." Richard Jones smiled as he stood up to greet the pair and gestured to the two chairs in front of his desk. Penny set a package down beside her chair and leaned forward. Her eyes were immediately drawn to the painting above his head.

"Now, Penny," he began, "stay with us here for the signing, and we'll chat about the other matter when we've wrapped up the real estate business." He peered at her over the top of his glasses. "You're investing a lot of money in this property, although I must say I was very pleased indeed to see you got it for considerably less than the asking price."

"It had been on the market for a very long time," Victoria explained, "and it's going to need a lot of work. We know that. The roof and guttering will be expensive, so the vendors had to take that into account. And lying empty for so long didn't improve its condition."

Jones nodded and then brought out the legal documents he had prepared.

"Well, if you're ready, let's get started." He looked from one to the other the way he always did. "I always think this process calls for a special ceremony of some kind to mark the occasion. Maybe I should have to wear a special hat or something."

"A nice blue velvet one with a gold tassel," suggested Penny. "Something to give it a medieval judicial look!"

They all smiled, and Jones pointed to the places on the documents where signatures were required. They worked in silence, except for the occasional light ripping sound as he peeled red and yellow SIGN HERE tabs from the papers.

A few minutes later, they all sat back in their chairs.

"Congratulations!" he said.

Victoria and Penny looked at each other, their smiles silted with anxious excitement.

"Yes, but it's a bit daunting, that's for sure," Victoria said. "We've just bought ourselves a derelict stone building beside the river. Still, wait until you see what we make of it!"

"I have no doubt you ladies will turn it into a charming, prosperous business." He replaced the signed papers in a large folder and stepped out from behind his desk. "And now I'd better get out of the way so Penny can get in here to look at the painting."

Penny came round behind him.

"Actually, Mr. Jones," she began, "I wanted to do more than just look at it. I wondered if you might lend me this painting for a few days. I'd like to have the time to really examine it, and if you wouldn't mind, I'd like to photograph it."

She hurried on.

"I know you wouldn't want your clients looking at an empty picture hook, so I brought you this painting to hang in its place." She pulled out the watercolour of the blowsy roses from Emma's flat. "I know it's not nearly as good, but just for a couple of days." Her earnest pleading seemed to amuse him.

"Yes, all right," he agreed after a moment. "I'm sure you appreciate how precious it is to us and I know you'll take good care of it. And just for a couple of days, mind. In fact, we should probably set a day for its return. You know perfectly well I wouldn't entrust it to anyone else. Shall we say Friday?"

Penny agreed and reached up to take down the painting. As she touched it, she felt a frisson of excitement ripple over her. She set it down carefully on the solicitor's desk, quickly removed the wrapping from the replacement painting, and hung it on the empty hook behind his desk.

Jones glanced at it, and then gave her a measured look.

"You should know, Penny, that my brother, Alun, is not happy with what you're doing. He thinks that our sister's death is a private, family matter best left alone, and he's uncomfortable that you're stirring all this up."

"How do you feel?" Penny asked softly.

146

Jones seemed to age before her eyes. His eyes misted and he turned away. He looked unseeing out the window at the street below.

"You know, people expect you to get over something like this, but you never do. You learn to live with it, that's all. All these years there's the pain of the loss and on top of that, the pain of not knowing. So much destroyed in one hideous moment. Someone took my sister's life and then just kept going as if nothing had happened, probably without so much as a backward glance."

He brought his gaze back to Penny's.

"If knowing who did this to her could help make some of that pain go way, then I'm all for it."

"No matter what the truth is?" Penny asked.

Jones nodded. "No matter."

With a small sigh, he straightened his shoulders and picked up their file.

"Right. Well, I think that's all for now. As you know, the vendors want a quick closing, so I think we can get all this paperwork done, and if you could come back next week, we'll hand over the keys. In the meantime, I think you should organize the builders and get the renovation work lined up."

Penny wrapped the Alys Jones picnic painting in the bubble wrap and brown paper that had protected the watercolour of the roses, and they said their good-byes.

When they were out on the street, Penny turned to Victoria. "Well, I think we learned one thing today," she said as they walked slowly toward the town square. "I don't think he had anything to do with it. Not that we ever thought he did, of course," she added quickly. "But why do you think Alun Jones doesn't want us to look into this? Do you think he's hiding something?"

"Maybe he doesn't want the lesbian relationship to come out?" Victoria suggested.

"That seems pretty weak these days," Penny said, "but you could be right." She thought for a moment. "If he feels that way about it today, maybe he didn't want it coming out thirty years ago, either. Maybe her parents didn't know, or he thought they'd be ashamed or embarrassed if it got out.

"Anyway, I can't wait to get this painting home, put it with the other, and see if they have anything to tell us."

Penny let herself into the cottage, walked through to the dining room, and set the painting down on the table. She returned to the living room, picked up the companion painting, and set it down on the table beside the first one. Then, she looked around for something to use to prop them up so she could view them better. She picked up a few books to lean them against, and then pulled a couple more off the bookshelf. She put them against the bottom of the frames, wedging the paintings into an upright position.

She sat down, crossed her arms on the table, and rested her chin on them. She looked from one painting to the other, drinking them in. She loved the way the paintings looked together and was filled with admiration for the artist. She was so young, Penny thought. Really just getting started. Imagine what she might have achieved had she lived and had another twenty, thirty, or forty years to develop and expand her craft and creativity. And, Penny thought as she felt the sting of unshed tears, there's love there. This artist loved these canvases.

Together, the paintings told one story. Individually, they told another. Penny tilted her head and looked more closely at the Jones painting. The figure of the woman, she was sure, was Emma. There was something about the way she held her glass of wine that looked so familiar. Penny had seen her holding an icy glass of gin and tonic on many a summer's day in exactly that way, using her left hand to steady the glass by supporting the bottom. The male figure, dressed in trousers and a vest, appeared very relaxed as he leaned toward the female figure. His shirt was open at the collar and he wasn't wearing a tie. A moment in time gone by, thought Penny. A guy on a picnic now would just as likely be wearing a ripped pair of jeans, scruffy T-shirt, and baseball cap on backward. She looked closer. Was it a man? Or was it Alys, wearing the same clothes she wore in that photograph taken in the art college staff lounge that had been printed in the *Liverpool Echo*?

And if the subjects in that painting were Alys and Emma, who was in the other paintings? Could the male figure be Andrew Peyton, and the female be either Cynthia Browning or Millicent Mayhew?

She gazed at the paintings, taking in the play of light on the figures and background. The artist had used her brush strokes confidently and yet sparingly and lightly to suggest the bank of purple flowers in the background. It was impossible to tell what kind they were. Bluebells? Forget-me-nots? Violets? But aren't violets a spring flower? These paintings had the look of high summer about them.

Where was this scene painted, Penny wondered. She had hiked and rambled on her painting excursions around much of the area, or so she thought, but she had no idea where this could be. She looked at the artist's signature on the bottom left of the painting: A. Jones. She would have loved to have stroked it but knew better than to touch the painting.

She sighed softly, looked at her watch, and realized she was starting to get hungry.

She went to the kitchen for a glass of water, but before she could sit down again, she was startled by a knock at the door. Her drinking glass shook slightly, spilling a few drops on the floor. She held the glass well away from the paintings on the table and looked around for a place to set it down.

The knocking came again, a little louder this time and, she imagined, more insistent. She set the glass down on a nearby table and headed for the door, wiping a damp hand on her trousers.

She braced herself, then opened the door.

"Hello," he said. "I know I should have called first, but I wondered if I might come in and have a word."

Penny stepped silently aside to let Gareth enter. He seemed somehow smaller than when she'd seen him last. She gestured at her sofa, and he sank into its squishy depths.

She sat near him, in one of the wing chairs, and pinched her lips together as she waited for him to speak. She could not meet his eyes and, instead, looked at her hands.

"I've missed you," he said simply. "I don't know what's

happened or what's gone wrong, but I must have done something to upset you. Whatever it was, I'm sorry, and I'm so hoping you'll give me the chance to make it up to you."

Penny turned her attention to a tree in the front garden, its leaves gently brushing against the diamond panes of the window.

She made a vague gesture with her hands.

"I don't know what to say to you, Gareth, except I'm sorry. I just don't think this is going to work."

He swallowed and patted the back of his neck.

"I was afraid you'd say that. I was thinking rather the opposite. I thought we could be really good together. Are you saying we shouldn't see each other again?"

Penny nodded. "I think I am. I just feel it would be for the best."

A heavy silence, tinged with frost and awkwardness, settled over them.

He reached out to her, but she withdrew her hand before he could touch it.

"I see," he said, and then stood up. He glanced around the room and seeing the two paintings propped up on the table, appeared about to say something and then thought better of it.

"Well, I'll leave you to it then. Good night."

She followed him to the door, opened it for him, and watched as he set off down the path. Look back at me, she thought. Look back. But he didn't and a few moments later she heard the sound of his car starting as she closed the door.

Heart pounding, she leaned against it. What have I done, she thought. Instead of feeling the relief she had expected, she felt an overwhelming sense of loss. She opened the door and looked out, but as twilight fell over her front garden, she knew there was no one there.

She walked back into her sitting room, and suddenly the paintings didn't seem quite so interesting and she realized she was no longer hungry.

Thirteen

The soft thud of the morning post landing on the rectory's hallway floor was the signal for Robbie to swing into action.

He raced down the hall, barking loudly, to warn off the unseen threat to the safety and well-being of his family that seemed to present itself most days about this time.

"The post has arrived," Bronwyn commented as she held up the coffeepot with a quizzical look at her husband.

"Yes, please," he said, as he rose from the table.

"All right, then, Robbie," he muttered as he made his way to the front door. "Come on now, there's a good boy."

Wagging his tail, Robbie charged ahead in the direction of the kitchen where his next task of the day awaited him: helping Bronwyn clear the plates.

The rector scooped up the morning post and followed the small dog back to the kitchen.

He placed the little pile in front of him and began to sort it. "Oh, here's a postcard from your sister," he said as he handed it to Bronwyn. "Where'd they go, again?"

"Arizona."

"Oh, right, Arizona. The weather's very good out there, I hear. Many pensioners take advantage of it. It's meant to be very dry or something like that."

He placed a few bills to one side and then looked at the two magazines that had just arrived.

He chose *Wales Today* and, after glancing over the index, turned a few pages and scanned the contents. A small article caught his attention and he started to read, then chuckle.

"What is it, dear?" asked Bronwyn.

"It's called bog snorkeling, of all things. Here, listen," and he read out loud: "'In Llanwrtyd Wells, crowds watch competitors swim up and down a hundred-and-thirty-three-meter bog filled with sulphurous, weedy water. Some wear silly costumes, but all entrants must not use conventional swimming strokes, relying on flipper power only.'"

He patted his stomach. "I think I should take it up. I expect I'd be a natural. And as you always like to remind me, I should take more exercise."

Smiling, Bronwyn got up from the table and came round to stand beside him. Leaning over his shoulder, she looked at the photograph and rocked with laughter.

"Oh! And we could get you a nice rubber suit. What with the flippers, you'd look so fetching I'd not be able to keep my hands off you."

154

They giggled together while he wrapped his arm around her waist.

A few moments later Bronwyn returned to her seat, and Thomas looked at the cover of his weekly *Church Times* bulletin. He riffled through a few pages and then turned to the obituaries.

"It's a sad commentary on our lives when we start to take an interest in the obituaries," he remarked to his wife, who was buttering her toast while she admired the image of a large cactus on the postcard that she had propped up against her juice glass.

"No one we know mentioned there, I hope."

The rector scanned the list.

"No, I don't think so. Wait. Who's this?"

He read for a few moments in silence.

"Bronwyn, listen to this! 'Suddenly, at his home in Llandudno, the Reverend William Peyton, in his seventy-ninth year. Survived by his wife, Marjorie, three children, six grandchildren, and brothers, Andrew and John.' And then it goes on about the funeral arrangements."

"I don't think we know him, do we, dear? Perhaps you met him in the course of your duties, but the name doesn't ring a bell with me."

"No, not him, Bronwyn. His brother. Andrew Peyton. Isn't that the name of the man Penny was interested in? The artist fellow from that group of people in Liverpool that are connected to Alys Jones?" He fumbled about in his pocket for his diary. "Let me see. Where did I write those names? Yes! Here we are—Millicent, hmmm, yes! Andrew Peyton! No, not an artist. He was the curator."

"But we don't know if it's the same fellow," his wife commented.

"No, but I'm sure Penny would want to know, anyway," he replied with mild impatience. "I must ring her right away. Excuse me for a moment."

Bronwyn spread a little more marmalade on her toast, then broke off a piece and slipped it to Robbie, who was sitting beside her chair.

"Hello, Penny," the rector was saying, "sorry to ring you so early but wanted to get you before you left for the shop.

"Sorry, salon. Anyway, I wondered if you fancied going to a funeral with us on Thursday morning in Llandudno."

He laughed.

"Yes, I know it seems a bit odd, but you know that Andrew Peyton fellow you were interested in? I don't know if this is the same one, but . . ." He read the contents of the obituary notice.

"Right, then, we'll pick you up at nine. See you then."

He set down the telephone receiver and returned to his wife.

"She was very keen to go."

"Of course she was! Like a dog with a bone, that one."

Robbie cocked his head.

"No, poppet, not you!"

The drive to Llandudno took them along twisting and turning rural roads that were so narrow in places they had to pull over so an oncoming car could pass. Bronwyn had decided not to go, saying poor Robbie would be absolutely bursting by the time they got home. When the rector had suggested that he would come to no harm tied up in the garden for a few hours, she had given him such a dark look he might as well have suggested that they have Robbie for dinner. Victoria had planned to go, but work was beginning on the spa renovation, and with Eirlys on her own at the salon, she felt she should stay behind in Llanelen, and reluctantly, Penny had to agree.

"So it'll just be the two of us, Penny," the rector had said. "As a fellow rector, it won't seem strange for me to attend the funeral, even though I never knew him, and maybe we can be vague about that bit, if we have to. But hopefully you'll learn something at the reception afterward."

They arrived at Holy Trinity Church in the centre of Llandudno just as the service was about to start. Nodding and smiling gravely at people they didn't know, they made their way down the centre aisle along the blue patterned carpet and found seats to the right, underneath a brilliant stained-glass window. Another time, Penny's mind would have drifted off while she studied and admired it, but today she barely took any notice of it, as her attention was riveted on the small group of mourners seated in the front pew.

Unfortunately, all she could see was the backs of their heads. She thought the small woman with the white hair and thin, frail shoulders must be Peyton's widow. On each side of her sat two burly men who appeared to be in their late forties—sons, perhaps? Her eyes moved down the row to the figure at the end of the row. An elderly man with thinning hair in an outdated brown pin-stripe suit held his hymn book in a steady hand, and when he turned slightly to his left, she could see a gauntly elegant profile whose contours had been softened by time. That's got to be him, she thought. That's Andrew Peyton.

Following the brief, oddly impersonal service, the small group of mourners moved into the church hall, where a modest spread had been laid out. Penny and the rector took a couple of limp cheese and cucumber sandwiches from the tray.

"Let's stay together when I talk to him," Penny said in a low voice. "You've seen a lot of human nature, and your impressions will really help." She grimaced. "I must admit I'm feeling a little nervous about this. I wish Bronwyn were here. She's really good at this sort of thing. She'd know what to say."

The rector nodded.

"I'll just pay my respects to Mrs. Peyton and be right back."

He drifted to the entrance of the hall, where Mrs. Peyton was receiving guests. Penny watched as he introduced himself. A gentle smile spread across her face, and she shook his hand warmly. The rector spoke to her for a few minutes and then said hello to the two men with her.

The man they thought was Andrew Peyton was at the tea table, so with a slight nod at Penny the rector glided off in that direction and she followed.

Penny found herself standing beside a tall, effete man. She watched his long, delicate fingers as he picked up the pitcher and poured a few drops of milk into his tea.

"Hello," said the rector. "I'm Reverend Thomas Evans from Llanelen, and this is my neighbour Penny Brannigan." The man looked from one to the other and smiled vaguely. "Hello," he said. While his accent was definitely English, Penny could not place it. It didn't sound Scouse, as it would have if he'd grown up in Liverpool.

"I wonder, now," said the rector smoothly, "if you would be William's brother Andrew?"

The man nodded.

"Did you know my brother?"

"Sadly, no, not personally," the rector said, fingering his clerical collar, "but, of course, in a professional capacity, as I live and work in a neighbouring parish, I wanted to come along today to pay my respects." Handing Peyton a business card, he introduced himself and Penny. "And, interestingly, we may have something in common. That is, Penny here might. Is it possible that you are the Andrew Peyton who was a curator of art in Liverpool in the 1960s? Penny is an artist, you see, and doing some research into that period."

Brilliant, thought Penny. He didn't mention Alys.

Peyton gave Penny an icy appraisal as he dropped the rector's business card into his jacket pocket without having bothered to look at it.

"Yes, I was associated with the Liverpool School of Art at that time," he said. "We did put on some rather good shows. Showcased new artists. Of course, there was a lot of great talent about to work with. Liverpool was in the midst of a renaissance, you might say, fueled by the music." He raised his teacup to his lips in an oddly feminine way. "The Mersey sound," he added sarcastically.

"I'd love to learn more about the period," Penny said, "and speak to one of the artists, Millicent Mayhew. She was one of your group, I believe. Could you put me in touch with her, do you think?"

Peyton dropped his gaze to the bottom of his now empty tea-cup, and then, as the cup clattered slightly, he set it on the table.

Rubbing his long fingers together, he turned to Penny.

"I'm not sure exactly where she is now," he said, "we lost touch some time ago. And now, if you'll excuse me, it's been a stressful day and I'd like to go home."

Penny nodded and stepped aside. She and the rector watched as he made his way across the room, said a few words to his sister-in-law, and then left the hall.

"Come on, Thomas," Penny said. "He's lying. We have to follow him or we might never find him again. Let's see where he goes."

The rector took a long, last draught of his tea and, with a sigh, set the cup down on the table beside Peyton's.

"Right. I'll just say good-bye to Mrs. Peyton and we'll be off."

They got into the rector's car just as Peyton pulled out of the parking lot. They followed him as he drove through the town, and then along Marine Drive, and when he switched on his right turn indicator, the rector did the same, turning into the Sunset Villas Retirement and Nursing Home.

"Oh, why do they always give these places awful names like that!" Penny moaned. "Sunset Villas, Gateway Haven . . ." She stopped as Peyton parked in a visitor's spot, got out of his car, and entered the building. "Can we park over there?" she asked, gesturing to an empty spot at the end of a row of cars, which gave them a good view of the entrance. The rector glanced at his watch. "Just for a few minutes, and then I'm afraid I have to get back to Llanelen." Penny nodded.

"Well, he's in a visitor's parking spot," she said, "so he doesn't live here. I wonder who does."

They sat in silence for a few moments, and then the rector remarked, "Mrs. Peyton said Andrew probably had to leave because it was time for his injection. Apparently he's diabetic, so if he needs his insulin, he shouldn't be in there too long. Still, it seems odd he would come here instead of going home. What on earth is he doing here if he should be taking care of his diabetes?"

They looked at each other in puzzlement, and then the rector, glancing at his watch, reached down and switched on the radio. They listened to the news on Radio 1 for a few minutes, and then with a long sigh, the rector switched off the radio. He patted his pockets, then turned to Penny.

"If you'll just excuse me for a moment, my dear, I think I'll just get out and stretch my legs for a minute or two. Maybe take a little stroll and admire the garden."

He sloped off and soon disappeared behind a tree. A few moments later, wisps of smoke drifted away from the tree, carried away on a light breeze.

He thinks Bronwyn doesn't know that he sneaks the occasional cigarette, Penny thought, as she chuckled to herself.

With a satisfied smile, the rector returned to the car, and just as he settled into his seat, the door of the building opened and Peyton emerged. With long, purposeful strides he walked to his car, started it up, and drove off.

"Do you want to go in and try to find out what he was doing here?" asked the rector.

"No, not today. I know you need to get home. But I'll bet

you anything that Millicent Mayhew lives here. I can confirm that by phone. And if she does live here, why did he deny knowing her? He said he'd lost touch with her." She thought for a moment. "When I do go to see her, I'll need a better idea of what I'm going to say." She turned to the rector and smiled. "It's interesting, though, that we didn't even mention Alys Jones and he heads straight over here. You were really good back there, by the way, with Peyton. What did you think of him?"

"I thought there was something decidedly shifty about him," the rector replied as he put the car in gear and they pulled out of the parking lot. At the end of the driveway he checked for oncoming traffic and then turned toward the long and winding road that would take them home. "He's either lying or hiding something. Or maybe both. And I think he was definitely nervous. You've put the wind up him, my dear."

Penny sighed and settled back in her seat. She looked out the window for a few minutes as the houses thinned out and gradually disappeared, giving way to lush green fields partitioned by stone fences that bound them together like grey ribbons.

"You know," the rector continued, "it really is too bad that Bronwyn couldn't come. She's a wonderful judge of character and not much gets past her. She would have had him figured out in no time."

He slowed down as a car filled with young people overtook them.

"Would you look at that! And on this narrow road. Honestly, everyone's in such a hurry nowadays. What in heaven's name is the matter with them?"

He shifted gears and glanced in his rearview mirror.

"Anyway, where was I? Oh, right, Bronwyn. She's really enjoying that little dog. Says she must have had a life before Robbie, but it couldn't have been up to much." He laughed lightly. "I wasn't sure how to take that."

From Penny's handbag came the sound of a mobile phone ringing. She pulled the phone out and checked who was calling.

"Sorry, Thomas, it's Victoria. She wouldn't ring unless it was important, so I should take this. Please excuse me."

"Go right ahead. You're not driving!"

"Hello?"

She listened for a moment.

"You've got to be kidding! No, no, I'm sorry, I don't know why I said that. Of course you're not kidding. Yes, we're on our way home now. We should be there in about, oh, forty-five minutes or so."

She listened again, then said a hurried good-bye and turned to the rector.

"You're not going to believe this, but the workmen have just found skeletal remains in the ductwork in the building we just bought. And the first day on the job, too!"

Fourteen

Penny's mobile rang again when they were about five minutes outside Llanelen. She answered it, made a few noises to indicate she was listening, and then rang off.

"Victoria just wanted me to know that Gareth has just arrived."

The rector made a noncommittal sound and then commented, "I'm not sure what that means—whether it's good or bad. Bronwyn won't tell me what's going on with you two, so I'm afraid I really don't know what to say."

Penny gave a little laugh that sounded more like a snort.

"Well, I don't know what there is to tell you, really. We were sort of together, but not really, if you know what I mean, but now we're not. Victoria just wanted me to know he was there, in case I felt awkward. Oh! I'd better let Eirlys know I'm delayed. If we can go straight to your house, I can easily walk to the building from there."

The rector nodded, and a few minutes later they pulled into his driveway. Bronwyn came out to meet them, Robbie at her heels.

"Whatever's happened?" she asked. "There's an awful lot of commotion over at the spa—police cars and everything. I hope nobody's been injured."

"I'd better get over there," Penny said. "Thomas will fill you in on what we know so far," she said to Bronwyn. "Oh, and Thomas, thank you so much for this morning. I really appreciate it."

"That's all right, my dear. Good luck with whatever it is you've got to be dealing with."

Penny bent down to give Robbie a little pat and then set off toward the stone building, which, in the space of a morning, had been transformed from a renovation project to a crime scene. Police cars with lights flashing and radio chatter crackling blocked access to the area, and uniformed police officers, backed up by yellow crime-scene tape, prevented the growing crowd of onlookers from getting too close.

At the edge of the perimeter, just outside the yellow tape, Victoria was reaching for her mobile when Penny hurried up to her.

"Oh, I'm so glad you're here," Victoria said. "This is unreal. They'd just begun work"—she pointed to a pile of boards with nails sticking out of them, rusted pipes, the cistern from an old toilet, and a broken chair—"when one of the men ap-

166

parently found a pile of bones in the ductwork. And we were just getting started!"

"That's exactly what I said!" replied Penny. "I guess Gareth is inside, is he? And we're not allowed to go in?"

"That's right."

"Do they know if the remains are human?"

"I didn't see them, but apparently from the look of them it's pretty obvious. Oh, and there's more, and you're really not going to like it."

"You mean I'm not going to like it any more than I like that there's a dead body in the ductwork of our new building?"

Victoria looked around and then lowered her voice.

"There are two skulls, the workman said. One he thought was human and the other was much smaller."

"Oh, no!" said Penny. "A child?"

Victoria shook her head. "It's not that shape. He thinks it might be a dog or cat."

Penny gasped. "You're right. I don't like it."

She glanced at her watch. "Right, well, you stay here and you can tell me everything that happens. If I hurry, I can just about make it back to the salon."

"You don't have to worry about the salon," Victoria assured her. "I had a word with Eirlys, and she's happy to carry on."

"I'm sure she is," Penny agreed, "but today's Thursday, so Mrs. Lloyd'll be coming in for her appointment. I want to take care of her myself so I can talk to her."

"Ah," said Victoria, getting it. "Pick her brain, you mean."

Penny shuddered.

"I hate that expression! But you were right when you suggested that Mrs. Lloyd would be a good source of information. I'll ask her today what she can remember about this building—she's got a memory like a steel trap that goes back a long way, and she was well aware of just about everything that went on."

Victoria nodded and Penny walked quickly back to the salon.

Eirlys, who was setting out bottles of nail varnish on the worktable, jumped when Penny walked through the door.

"Oh, Penny! We've just heard the news about the discovery of the dead bodies in the new spa. Really shakes you up, when something that awful can happen here."

Penny nodded as she set down her handbag.

"Now, Eirlys, you're not to worry yourself over this. I'm sure it happened a long time ago—before you were even born, probably—so you're as safe as houses. No one's going to hurt you, I promise. Now, Mrs. Lloyd will be coming in soon, and I'm going to do her nails myself today. So I'd like you to take your break now. Did you have lunch?"

Eirlys nodded.

"Victoria came in and closed the shop over the lunchtime."

"Well, then, why don't you text a friend and see if you can meet up for coffee for an hour or so." She checked the appointments book. "Then, when you come back, we'll finish up for the afternoon. The discovery at the new building could very well affect us all over the next few days."

With an obliging nod, Eirlys went through to the back and collected her bag. As she passed through the salon on the way to the door, she gave Penny a worried look.

"Do you think this business at the spa will mean we can't open? I know you and Victoria wanted the place open by Christmas. Will this delay things, do you think?"

"It might, for a day or two, but I'm sure Inspector Davies will have it all sorted quickly, and really, once the body has been taken away, there's nothing to stop us from getting on with the renovations, is there?"

"No, I guess not," said Eirlys as she opened the door. "But clients might not want to come there because of this. They might find it too weird and creepy."

Penny gave a light, ironic laugh.

"Oh, I think you'll find it will work quite the opposite way, Eirlys. You know what people are like. They'll want to come to the spa because of what happened there."

As Eirlys was about to leave, Mrs. Lloyd burst in, her eyes radiating intense excitement.

"Oh, Eirlys, love, are you leaving?"

"Yes, Mrs. Lloyd, but I've left out a few bottles of nail varnish that I think you'll like, for you to choose from."

"Oh, that's lovely, dear. So thoughtful of you. Thank you so much." She set down her bag and eased herself into the client's chair. "Now, then, Penny," she said eagerly, when Eirlys had closed the door quietly behind her, "you must tell me everything about what's going on at the new site this morning. I hear a body's been discovered! Who could it possibly be? Not anyone we know, surely!"

"I'm afraid I really don't know too much about it," Penny said as she picked up Mrs. Lloyd's hand and began to shape her nails. "Victoria is there now, and I expect after she's spoken to the police she'll be able to tell us a bit more, so we'll just have to wait to hear from her." Mrs. Lloyd pinched her lips together but said nothing.

"And of course, your niece Morwyn will be there for the *Daily Post,* so I expect she'll be asking all the right questions and will know more than anybody. She'll have to, won't she, if she's going to write about it."

Mrs. Lloyd nodded.

Penny got up from the table and returned a few minutes later with the soaking bowl, which she offered to Mrs. Lloyd.

Mrs. Lloyd dipped her fingers in the soaking bowl, and this time, perhaps because her mind was elsewhere, did not complain the water was too hot.

"Mrs. Lloyd, I'd like to ask you about something," Penny began. "You've lived in this town all your life and you know it better than just about anybody. I wondered if you'd tell me what you can remember about our building. The new spa."

Mrs. Lloyd gave her a shrewd look and then chuckled.

"Have you heard of horses and barn doors, Penny? The time to be asking me about the building was before you bought it, not after!"

"Yes, you're right as usual, Mrs. Lloyd," Penny said contritely. "But tell me everything you can remember about it. What it's been used for and who owned it. And when."

"Well, let me see." Mrs. Lloyd thought for a moment.

"When my mother was a girl, and that's going back a ways, it was some kind of inn or hostelry. It even had stables, I think. And then, during the war they used to billet soldiers there, because they took them up into the hills for training. Then, in the 1950s, I think it was a youth hostel, and in the 1960s and '70s it was filled with hippies and squatters, and I think it's pretty much been empty since then. Oh, people have talked from time to time about fixing it up, but nothing ever came of that, until you and Victoria decided to take it on.

"Are you sure you know what you're doing, by the way? Did you get some good advice?" She mulled that over and then answered the question herself. "Well, apparently not or you wouldn't have bought a building with a dead body in it, would you?"

She picked up each of the nail polishes Eirlys had set out for her and, after a bit of wavering back and forth, settled on a rich burgundy.

Penny dried Mrs. Lloyd's hands and, unwrapping a sterile packet of clippers, started trimming her cuticles.

"I wonder who it is," Mrs. Lloyd mused. "Or was. It's sad that, isn't it?"

Penny looked up at her, the clippers poised in mid-air. "What is?"

"Well, when people go missing. Sometimes their relatives wait in vain for word, but the bodies are never found. Or maybe they're found years later. Maybe even after a parent has died. Very sad, that, if it's a young person." Penny nodded and they sat in silence for a moment until Mrs. Lloyd was ready to continue.

"But sometimes people just disappear, and no one knows they're gone and no one misses them. People who are estranged from their families and have no friends. They're dead, but no one knows they're dead. They might just as well have moved to another city, or even moved to another country, for that matter. Who knows? Who cares? No one."

Penny felt a chill and shuddered.

"Yes, it's getting cooler now," Mrs. Lloyd went on. "Autumn is almost here, and it'll be Christmas before we know it." She sniffed and held her arm out to admire her nails, as she always did.

"Looks nice. I guess I do tend to favor the burgundies, especially with autumn closing in. I had that awful pink, that time, do you remember? It looked like a strawberry milkshake! This is much more suitable. I don't know how you let me choose that pink!"

She sighed and watched as Penny went on with her work.

"Well, I've been wondering how you're getting on with fixing up Emma's cottage. You must miss her. Emma wasn't the soft lady everyone thought she was, you know. She had quite a head for business and investments, and you didn't want to argue with her. She always liked to have the last word, Emma did."

Penny nodded. "Yes, and she was usually right. She knew a lot about a lot of things. As for the cottage, I'm afraid I've been very slow with it. Cleared out a few things, but not her bedroom, yet."

She gave a little gasp. "Oh, no. I promised Bronwyn things for the jumble sale, and I haven't even started the bedroom. I'll have to get to that this weekend."

She finished applying Mrs. Lloyd's topcoat.

"There you go! All done."

Just as Mrs. Lloyd was about to reply, the door opened and her face lit up.

"Oh, hello!" she said. "Look, Penny, it's that nice policeman of yours. He'll have some news for us, no doubt. I'd better just sit here if you don't mind, while my nails dry. I wouldn't want anything to happen to them."

Fifteen

ello, Penny." Detective Inspector Gareth Davies smiled at one woman and then the other. "Mrs. Lloyd." Penny had turned in her chair and, in the awkwardness of the moment, started to rise.

"Now, Penny," said Mrs. Lloyd, "why do you look so surprised to see the inspector? He's investigating a dead body that's been found in a building you own, so of course he's going to come and talk to you."

But before coming to the salon, he had had a word with Victoria. Victoria had watched as he ducked under the yellow police tape and started walking toward his car. When she'd called his name, he turned round and, seeing who it was, smiled and waited for her to catch him up.

"Oh, Gareth," Victoria said, "before we get into all this

business"—she tossed her head in the direction of the building—"I just want to tell you I'm so sorry about what's happened with you and Penny. Listen, I think she cares about you, but she's confused. You need to talk to her and get things sorted out."

"I did talk to her and she pretty much told me to get lost."

"Well, from what I've heard, you haven't talked about everything," Victoria said, making little quotation marks with her fingers around the word "everything."

"What are you talking about?"

"Look, I might as well tell you. I saw you coming out of the Red Dragon Hotel about a week ago early one morning with another woman."

"And you told her this?"

"I thought she would want to know."

"So she thinks that I . . ." His voice trailed off.

"Yes, she does."

"Oh, God! That was . . . never mind. Where's Penny now, do you know?"

"At the salon," Victoria replied.

"Right."

"But before you go," Victoria said, "please tell me what's happening here."

"We've processed the scene and we'll be removing the remains soon." He looked at his watch. "It's getting a bit late in the day now, but I would think that your workmen should be back on the job by tomorrow afternoon. We don't want to hold up work any longer than we have to."

He smiled and touched her arm.

"Thanks for telling me. I need to go and see her. I can put this right."

176

And so, a few minutes later he found himself in the salon, anxious to speak to Penny, but faced with Mrs. Lloyd, he knew that what he was aching to say would have to keep.

"Yes, we found skeletal remains in the building," he told the two women. "No, we don't know who or even how old they are. They'll be examined and we should know more soon. As far as the renovating goes, we should be out of your way by tomorrow, and work can resume."

"Is that it?" a disappointed Mrs. Lloyd asked. "Is that all you have to tell us?"

Davies lifted a shoulder slightly and turned over his hand in a deprecating gesture.

"That's all I have at the moment," he said, and let it go at that. Mrs. Lloyd, an experienced gossip, knew that if she kept silent, sooner or later he'd start talking to fill the silence. But she was no match for him. The silence stretched on while Mrs. Lloyd looked at him, then looked at Penny, then looked at her nails. Gareth caught Penny's eye and when he saw the faintest twitch of a smile at the corner of her mouth, he thought his bruised heart would melt. He smiled at her and she cleared her throat.

"Right, well, Mrs. Lloyd, I think your nails should be dry enough now," Penny said diplomatically. "I'm afraid I'm going to have to close up so I can get down to the site and check up on Victoria. It's been a long day for her."

Accepting defeat in a good-natured way, Mrs. Lloyd got to her feet, making a great show of being careful not to touch her nails.

"If you'll just get my bag for me, Penny," she said, and a few minutes later Davies was closing the door quietly behind her. He turned to face Penny, who picked up the towel from the worktable and started toward the back of the shop with it. He took her gently by the arm.

"Leave it for a moment and sit down. Please." For an instant he feared she would break away from him, but then he felt her relax under his grip as she folded herself back into her chair. He sat down across from her, and they looked at each other across the worktable.

"Thank you. Now, I need to tell you something, and I want you to just listen to me. I think you've got the wrong end of the stick. Apparently you've heard that I was leaving the Red Dragon Hotel the other morning with another woman, and you think that I . . ." He paused as she picked up a bottle of nail varnish and rotated it slowly. "Penny, it wasn't what you think it was.

"I was with a detective sergeant who happens to be an expert on counterfeit money. There's a lot of it about at the moment, and we'd had a call from the hotel about some bogus twenty-pound notes. So we had a little chat with Mrs. Geraint, and then we left. I wanted to stop in and see you, but Bethan called and we had to go to a farm on the other side of Betws y Coed. More agricultural bother. So that's all it was."

Penny bit on her lower lip and then finally brought her eyes to meet his.

"Did you really think I could do something as stupid as that, feeling the way I do about you?" he asked. "I wake up every morning, and the first thing I think about is you. I wonder if I'm going to see you that day. I try to find ways to run into you. You have no idea how much I want to put things right between us."

He looked at her with a mixture of fear and hope in his eyes.

"Well? Say something. Are we good?"

He waited for a moment, and then, this time, he did move in to fill the silence.

"What am I looking at?" Davies asked, turning the photo over to read the writing on the back. Penny stood very close to him, looking at the photo over his arm, and then took it away from him.

"If you'd come to Liverpool with me," she began. He winced.

"If you'd come to Liverpool with me, you'd know that Alys was part of a group of influential and up-and-coming 1960s artists that included Millicent Mayhew and Cynthia Browning. Also part of that circle was a curator called Andrew Peyton. I found this photo on the first day I was here." She lost herself for a moment in the black-and-white image, the woman in her dark mini dress with the white buttons, holding the fox terrier puppy.

"I thought it was a photo of Emma. Who can tell after thirty or forty years? People change. And everyone looked like that in the sixties. The hair, the clothes, the makeup. But now I think this is Cynthia Browning. It looks like the same woman in the *Liverpool Echo* photograph. And I know this is a big leap, but I am wondering if the remains of this woman and that poor little dog are the ones that were found today in the spa building."

She paused and touched his arm.

"At first, I thought it was Emma," Penny repeated, "but now I think she was the one who took the photograph."

Davies nodded. "Yeah. Could be. But it's a huge leap to connect a hit-and-run from decades ago to the body we found today."

"Well, it shouldn't be too hard to establish the connection, if there's one to be made, when your forensics people tell you if the bones are male or female and how old they are." She shrugged. "We'll just have to wait and see, I guess."

Smiling up at him, she added, "Do you know who lived on that street, by the way?" She responded to his blank look by telling him. "Only John Lennon. At number two fifty-one. The house was called Mendips."

"We can ask Merseyside police to help," Davies said. "Look, do you mind if I keep this for a bit?"

Penny shook her head. "No, you take it."

"Have you come across anything else I should know about?"

She pointed at the ceiling. "I haven't been through Emma's bedroom yet, but I have to do it soon. Bronwyn wants things for the annual harvest jumble sale. You're good at that sort of thing—going through people's effects. You do it all the time. I don't suppose you'd give me a hand with it, would you?"

Davies glanced at his watch.

"I suggest we leave Emma's room until morning. It's easier to do that sort of thing in daylight, and a few more hours shouldn't make a difference. But, for now, I'm going back to the building site to give Bethan a hand with the wrapping up—shouldn't be too long. May I take you to dinner after that? We've got some catching up to do."

"I'd be good with that," Penny replied. "And listen, I'm sorry I doubted you. I shouldn't have."

"It's okay," Davies said. "I understand. We're just getting to know each other. And I learned a long time ago that things are not always what they seem."

"So you'll be back for me in what, about an hour?"

"Yeah, if that's all right with you?"

"You know, I think I'll come with you. Could you drop me off at the flower shop? Then I'll walk over to the site, and we'll meet up there and then go for dinner."

"Great. Ready to go?"

"Almost. I just want to get a phone number."

Penny paused for a moment to take in the cool beauty of the lilies, roses, and carnations as they stood in their ugly buckets waiting to be plucked from their refrigerated unit and turned into beautiful arrangements. But something about a flower shop's heady fragrance always reminded her of a funeral.

"Hello," said the girl behind the counter. "I'm going to be closing up soon. Is there anything special I can help you with this evening?"

Why would she even mention closing the shop, Penny thought, when there's a customer standing right in front of her?

"Hmm. Possibly. I'm hoping you'll do something for me. Would you please ring this retirement home in Llandudno and say you have a floral delivery and are calling to confirm that a Millicent Mayhew is a resident there?"

The girl took the piece of paper, eyed it suspiciously, and gave a thoughtful chew on a hefty wad of gum.

"Why don't you ring it yourself?"

"Because they probably have call display, and when they see it's a florist, they'll tell you what I want to know." At that point, she could feel the niceness draining out of her. And because I'm the customer, I'm here to buy flowers, and I asked you to do it, she thought. What was it with shop assistants these days that made them think they had the right to insult their customers?

She had a sudden flashback to the Eaton's department store of her Canadian youth. No one at Eaton's would have spoken to a customer like that.

The girl hesitated and brushed the hair out of her eyes in a desultory way.

"I'm thinking about sending her a dozen roses," Penny remarked.

The girl sighed, picked up her telephone, dialed the number, spoke briefly, and then replaced the receiver.

"She lives there," the girl said.

"Do you know, I think I've changed my mind. I don't think I'll send those roses after all," Penny said. "I'll take them with me, if you wouldn't mind wrapping them up."

Penny left the shop with her purchase, making a mental note to have a word with the shop's owner. She'd want to know how her customers are being spoken to. I know I would. Oh, dear God, thank you for sending us Eirlys, she thought.

By the time she reached the spa building, the ribbon had

182

fallen off the flowers, the paper wrapper was soaked through at the bottom, and the cello tape had come undone at the top.

Most of the crowd had seen all there was to see and moved on, and although the crime-scene tape was still in place, the police cars were gone, taking with them the sense of drama and urgency.

She introduced herself to a tired and bored-looking uniformed officer, who waved her through into the building where Gareth was waiting for her at the entrance.

"Victoria's gone home," he said. "Said something about being desperate for a bath. Crime scenes often take people that way." He smiled at her. "I expect you'd like to see where we found the remains." In response to her quizzical look, he added, "It's all right. The crime-scene people have finished. There wasn't much to work with after twenty years or so."

The cement floor was littered with jagged lengths of broken boards, dusty cider bottles, piles of crumpled newspapers, an old shoe, a couple of filthy T-shirts, empty paint cans, and bits and pieces of metal work.

"The workers pulled out the ductwork and discovered the bones," Davies explained. "It looked as if the body had been placed inside and then the grille replaced. We'll know more when we've dated and typed the bones and determined what the building was being used for at that time."

Penny bent over and peered into the dark, empty space.

"Not much to see, is there?"

She straightened up and looked around. "What a huge mess. And the smell!"

Davies pointed at the flaking ceiling. The plastering had come away, exposing bare wood.

"Not sure if I should ask this, but are you sure you and Victoria can manage this renovation? Do you have any experience with this kind of project?"

"I don't, but Victoria does. She and her ex-husband did up properties in London and sold them. Made a lot of money. That's why her divorce settlement was tied up for so long." She sighed. "But I know what you mean. Still, the building inspectors tell us the place has good bones," she glanced at him, "so to speak. We're practically building it all new, so when we're done, it'll be something else. You wait and see."

"I believe you, though thousands wouldn't. Right, how about that dinner? What do you feel like tonight?"

"Hmm. The Barley Bin, I think. I fancy something hearty with mashed potatoes."

"Sounds good. Shall we go?"

"Just one more thing."

Penny walked over to the hole where the body had been found and gently laid the red roses on the floor in front of it.

"Of course, if the body is that of Cynthia Browning, we may have some problems finding any relatives," Davies said as the waiter brought them each a glass of wine. "Her parents are probably long dead. If people thought she emigrated, she would never have been reported as missing. And after all this time, there may be a problem obtaining dental records, but if she is who you think she is, Merseyside police will be glad to help, I'm sure."

"What will you do if it turns out not to be Cynthia Browning?" Penny asked. She helped herself to a bread roll, broke it in half, buttered it, and popped it in her mouth.

"We'll learn what we can from the remains and then search missing persons records for the right time frame. But that's business. Let's talk about something else."

"There is one thing I'd like to know," Penny said. "Why didn't you want to go with me to Liverpool? I thought we could have made a nice day of it."

Davies looked away and grimaced.

"I didn't think about it like that until later, and of course you're right, we could have." He shrugged. "I don't know what to say, really. It's just that when you asked, I didn't feel like going to Liverpool. Later, of course, I wished I had, but by then it was too late. I don't know if it was the drive or what, but I . . . I'm sorry, I know this is sounding hopelessly lame. It wasn't that I had anything better to do. And it certainly wasn't that I didn't want to be with you."

He gave her a soft smile.

"What did you do that afternoon, if I may ask?"

"You know, I can't remember. I expect I worked in the garden and took a nap."

Penny laughed.

"And how far off is your retirement, did you say?"

They settled back in their chairs and, when their salads arrived, tucked in.

A few minutes later, Penny picked up the conversation where they'd left off.

"I am going back to Liverpool, though, you might be interested to know. There's a multimedia exhibit opening soon of mid-twentieth-century Liverpool artists, and Victoria and I were planning to go. But I've been thinking about it—and I think you'll find the next bit rather clever—originally, we were just going to go to the exhibit, but now I want to go to the opening, because I reckon if there's anybody around from that time, they'll be invited, and I want to know who they are and to talk to them."

She gave him a sideways nod, with raised eyebrows.

"Well?"

When he leaned forward with a smile, she realized he had thought she was asking him to accompany her. She held up her hand and smiled.

"And no, I'm not asking you to go with me. Victoria and I are going, and we're going to treat ourselves to a good time. We might even stay overnight, maybe at the Adelphi."

He made a little gesture with a clenched fist. "Well, I am sorry I didn't take you to Liverpool. I guess I just didn't get it. Men are like that. You have to put the dots really close for us, so we can connect them. And that evening when I came round to you to try to sort all this out, I should have brought a peace offering. Flowers or chocolates. Sorry."

Penny finally had to laugh.

"Enough with the apologies. You didn't do anything wrong. Let's move on."

Davies paid the bill and they left the restaurant as dusk was falling. A grey gloom, heavy with the hint of damp autumn chill, was seeping through the streets. She tucked her arm in his, and they walked silently to his car.

"I'll bring some boxes in the morning and we'll make a start on the bedroom," he said as he parked outside the cottage a few minutes later. "I'll have to come early, say eightish, and I can only stay for a couple of hours."

Penny nodded. "We can get a lot done in two hours. I'll see you in the morning. Thank you." She reached out to him, and he pulled her into him. He held her for a few minutes, and then let go.

"I love the way you smell," she whispered. "Like a garden after the rain."

He watched as she entered the cottage, and when the light came on in the sitting room, he drove off.

Sixteen

enny awoke early the next morning, made herself a cup of coffee, which she set on a small tray, and headed back upstairs. She had barely been able to bring herself to set foot in Emma's bedroom since the afternoon she had moved in. But soon, once the personal things were cleared out, the room would be ready to be decorated and she could move into it. She was starting to feel ready.

She set the little tray down on the heavy, old-fashioned mahogany dresser and then glanced at the closet, where most of the things to be bundled up for the jumble sale would be.

She opened the closet door to find a few church-type hats on the shelf, half a dozen shoe boxes stacked neatly on the floor, and a predictable collection of dresses, blouses, and skirts. She moved them idly along the rail and then stepped back as a faint odor of powdery lavender hit her. At the end of the row of clothes was a zippered garment bag. She undid the zipper and peered in.

It contained what looked like a man's suit with a light-coloured dress or blouse tucked in behind it. She lifted the bag from the closet and laid it on the bed so she could examine it more closely. She pushed the edges of the bag back and then decided to take the suit out.

It was navy blue and, she thought, expensively tailored. She opened the jacket to see if there was a label. JACKSONS' THE TAILORS.

But something about the suit seemed odd. She held it up against her and realized she would have a hard time fitting into it, and, in fact, it would probably be too small for her to even try. She'd never get the trousers done up!

The bedsprings creaked as she sat down beside the garment bag, tenderly holding the suit in her arms. It had to have belonged to Alys. She carefully removed the jacket from the hanger and, placing it on her lap, ran her hand gently over a sleeve, feeling the soft finish of the smooth fabric. She fingered the lapels and hesitated as her hand reached the pockets. She checked both of them and was disappointed to find them empty.

But the bag had held two garments, and laying the suit on the bed, she pulled out the other item. It was a woman's sleeveless summer shirtwaist dress, belted, with a full skirt and a single row of small white buttons down the front. It had been white but was now starting to take on a yellowish hue.

But what caught Penny's attention was its delicate pattern of violets. In some places, just a single flower, in others, a few flowers tied together to form a posy.

She felt a sudden flood of relief that Gareth was on his way to help her deal with whatever secrets this room was about to give up. She laid the dress on the bed beside the suit, walked over to the dresser, and took a sip of tepid coffee. She heard herself making a little sound of distaste and set the cup down. She wandered over to the window and, glancing down into the garden, wondered where she would find the time to keep that up. It seemed like ages since she had sat out there with Gareth on her first day in the cottage, and since that day the garden seemed to have become even more tangled and unruly. She was starting to realize how much work and upkeep even a small property like this entailed. There would always be something that needed replacing, repairing, or polishing. For the first time she wondered how Emma had managed so apparently effortlessly to keep everything always looking so nice and still have time to teach school and enjoy a social life.

As far as Penny knew, Emma hadn't used any outside help, but she was starting to think she needed to hire someone to help her with the gardening and cleaning, especially now that the spa was going to be demanding so much of her time.

A knock at the front door interrupted her thoughts, and she ran down the stairs to open it.

"Hi," he said, setting down a couple of boxes. "Sorry I'm a bit late. Is there any coffee?"

"There is, but it's not very good, I'm afraid. I need to get a proper coffeemaker and maybe even a grinder for the beans."

"Well, whatever you've got will do for now. Shall I go on up?"

"Yes, why don't you make a start, and I'll be up in a few minutes with fresh coffee."

She watched Davies climb the stairs, and then she headed for the kitchen. A few minutes later, with two cups of coffee, she joined him.

"What do you think?" Penny asked.

"I think we're going to have to be ruthless. Shall we start with the clothes? Are you interested in the clothes? I think they're the easiest things to get rid of. You probably don't want to wear something she used to wear, but someone else, who doesn't know where they came from, will be glad to have them."

Penny nodded and pointed to the suit and dress on the bed.

"Except for those two. I'll put them back in the bag and hang on to them."

Gareth nodded.

"So let's get everything out of the closet. We'll fold up the clothes so we can get more in a box, and I'll drop them off at the rectory, if you like."

"That sounds perfect."

"Oh, and be sure to check the pockets. You never know what you'll find there."

"Right."

They worked their way through the contents of the closet but found nothing of interest. Shoes, hats, blouses, and skirts were soon packed up. Penny felt lightened to see them go. Gareth had been right. It was easy getting rid of these things that had no meaning to her. She opened the dresser drawers and bagged up underwear for the rubbish. In just over an hour, with only the occasional word exchanged between them, all Emma's personal effects had been removed. Penny had set aside the jewellery to go over more carefully, and the few prints on the wall had been added to the pile for the jumble sale. They looked at the bed and then at each other.

"What are you going to do about the furniture?" Gareth asked.

"I'm getting rid of all of it. Then I'm getting the room painted and filled with lovely new things."

Penny walked over to him, and just as she put her arms around his neck, his mobile rang.

"Oh, no," he said. They sat down on the bed while he answered it. He listened for a few seconds, nodded once or twice, and then rang off. He placed the phone in his jacket and looked at Penny.

"Sorry, love, duty calls."

He stood up and gave the room the once-over.

"I think we did a good job here. There's just the bedding left to do, I guess. You'll probably throw out the pillows, but you might want to wash the coverlet and donate it to the women's shelter, maybe?"

"Good idea," said Penny, as she pulled the coverlet down.

As she did so, she noticed the small paperweight sitting on the nightstand. She picked it up, liking the way its smooth coolness filled her hand.

"I don't think it's very valuable, but what makes it so wonderful is that I think it was a gift from Alys to Emma." She looked up at him. "Emma probably touched this every day of her life."

Gareth put his arms around her.

"I'll ring you later. Is your little group coming over this evening?"

Penny gave him a startled look.

"Oh, it's Friday! I'll have to speak to Victoria and see what we're doing. I guess they are coming over!" An idea flashed through her mind.

"Would you join us? Maybe you could update us on the bones found at the spa."

"Too early for that. We won't have the results for a couple of weeks at least, I would think. But I'll drop in. Say, about eight? Now, I must be off and you, too, I expect. I'll take the boxes with me so at least they're out of your way."

He clattered off down the stairs with one of the boxes, and Penny followed him with another. They loaded them in the car, and Penny waved him off. She watched his car disappear and then walked back into the cottage. She looked at her watch and, although she knew she should be leaving for the salon, picked up the telephone and left a message for Eirlys that she would be late.

She reached into her pocket and pulled out the paperweight. She thought about the memories it held and was surprised by the emotion it evoked in her. She felt deep sadness for all that had been lost and longed to know and understand what had happened and why.

She walked over to the table where the paintings were and set the paperweight down in front of them. Inanimate objects, but they had all been connected to something powerful. But what, exactly? Penny was now convinced that Alys had been murdered. Was there a connection to the bones in the spa? She felt impatient with how slowly things seemed to be moving.

Who would be the most likely to have some answers? The answer had to be Andrew Peyton. She knew from the police file that Bethan had left behind on that first night that he had been interviewed at the time of the accident, but he hadn't been very cooperative. But sometimes people mellow over time, and if he had information then that he was unwilling to reveal, he might be willing to talk about it now.

Resolving to track down Peyton, she made a light lunch and was just about to leave the cottage when the telephone rang. She hesitated before answering it. It was probably Victoria calling to ask about something, and she could ring her when she got to the salon. But something drove her to answer it.

"Hello?"

She spoke to the caller for a few minutes and then, just before the conversation ended, asked if she could ask just one question.

"Did the exhibition at the Walker Gallery go ahead?"

Thanking the caller, she rang off, and after applying a quick streak of lipstick, she let herself out of the cottage and walked quickly down the lane.

Anxious though she was to meet Victoria, she decided she should pop into the salon for a few minutes to see how Eirlys was doing.

She needn't have worried. As she opened the door, Eirlys and her client looked up and smiled at her. As Penny entered the salon, she recognized immediately that something was different, and when she took a closer look at the client, she realized what it was.

The client was a teenager, and the two young women had brought an atmosphere of lightness, energy, and fun to the salon.

"Penny, could I have a word, please?" asked Eirlys. Penny stepped into the small preparation area and Eirlys followed.

"It's about the nail varnish colours. We need more bright pinks and different colours, like yellow and silver. It's what the girls want." Penny looked into her eager, shining face and smiled. You can't put a price on enthusiasm, she thought.

"Yes, we certainly do!" she agreed. "Tell you what. I'm going to Llandudno this afternoon, so I'll pick up a few at the beauty supplier. You can tell me if I'm on the right track. But for today, will you be all right with what we've got?" Eirlys nodded and returned to her client.

"Hey, Jude, Penny says we're going to get some colours in!" she said. "I told you she'd be cool with it."

Penny smiled to herself and left to meet Victoria at the site.

An hour later, the two women were walking through the green fields that led to the next town, where they would catch the bus to Llandudno. They could have gone to the Watling Street stop in town but decided that the twenty-minute walk through the peaceful countryside would help them focus their thinking and give them time to discuss what they would say to Andrew Peyton when they met him.

"Tell me what he said," Victoria demanded. "You must have been gobsmacked when you picked up the phone and it's none other than Andrew Peyton!"

"I was just thinking about him," Penny replied. "It's odd how that happens sometimes, isn't it? I was just thinking about him and the phone went and it was him. I was that surprised I actually had to sit down.

"Anyway, he said he got my number from Thomas Evans, and could I come and see him. He asked if it would be possible to come today."

Victoria shot her a quizzical look.

"I know. And he apologized that it was on such short notice but said he wanted to tell me something about Alys, so of course I agreed."

She smiled at her friend.

"And it's really good of you to give up your afternoon to come with me."

Victoria stifled a yawn. "Well, what are friends for? And to think I could have been at home sneaking in a nap!"

"But I did manage to get in the question about the exhibit," Penny continued. "You know, the February exhibit at the Walker Gallery. And he said that no, with Alys's death, the exhibit did not go ahead. He said he didn't want to answer my questions over the phone and he'd talk to me when we got there. I'm hoping he might know where her paintings ended up."

They strolled on, admiring the sheep that grazed peacefully on each side of them. Penny loved and admired the hills that stretched higher and higher, cradling the valley. How many words are there for green, she wondered. Whatever the best one is, it must have been invented in Wales, for nowhere on Earth was there green like this.

Soon they came to the little pub that signaled they had almost reached the neighbouring town. Penny glanced at the letterbox outside the pub and, because it seemed to be almost in the middle of nowhere, wondered if anybody ever used it.

"I daren't even post my letters to you from the town post office—the post mistress is that nosey. I have to walk halfway to the next town and use the rural box outside the pub."

They walked on for a few more minutes until the Trefriw Mills bus stop came into view. About ten minutes later the bus arrived, and they hopped on, paid their fares, and found seats. The windows were rather dirty, and they had a difficult time seeing out.

The bus wound its way toward Llandudno, eventually skirting the majestic strength that is the thirteenth-century Conwy Castle, until it arrived at its final stop, the Llandudno Palladium. Deciding to leave the beauty-supply shop errand until later, they strolled the short way to Church Walks, stopping occasionally to admire something in a shop window. In minutes they arrived at the busy street at the foot of the Great Orme that stretches almost from the famous Victorian pier to the cable car station. Home to the occasional pub, the street was comprised mainly of guesthouses catering to summer tourists, most of whom had now departed. Victoria glanced at a piece of paper, scanned the street for the address Peyton had given Penny on the phone, and then pointed at the house they were looking for.

Three stories tall, painted a pale yellow with flower boxes on every window, it was probably built as the summer home for the family and servants of a prosperous Liverpool merchant. By the mid-twentieth century it would have been used as a bed-and-breakfast and within the last decade or so had been converted into small flats. Penny and Victoria climbed the steep stairs to the front door and looked at the names written on slips of paper beside doorbells. B. DOYLE. L. KENT. A. PEYTON. M. TUCKER.

Penny pushed the button beside Peyton's name, and they waited for a response. She checked her watch and then rang the bell again. When there was still no answer, she tried the door handle but it was locked. They stood on the step looking about and considering what to do when the door opened and a woman emerged, carrying a protesting cat in a large carrier case.

Penny grabbed the door, pulled it wide open, and stood to one side so the woman could pass. "Here you are." Penny smiled at her.

"Oh, thank you," the woman replied. "Just off to the vet. Such a bother it is. And with all the stairs, too."

Penny nodded, and they watched as the woman set off down the street, the cat yowling louder with every jostle of his cage. Then Penny and Victoria slipped into the building.

They found themselves in a small, dark foyer that smelled of yesterday's curry. A few shafts of desultory light filtered in over the transom, revealing a dark green carpet that led down a hall on the left and to a staircase on the right.

With a quick glance at each other, they wandered down the hall, past a heavy table, looking at the cream-coloured doors. "Peyton's elderly," Penny whispered, "so I expect he lives on the ground floor." Victoria nodded. Penny crept up to the first door and pressed her ear against it. She could hear what sounded like a radio playing pop music but couldn't make out the words. She shook her head, and they moved on to the next door.

As Penny knocked on it, the door slowly opened a few inches. With the tips of her fingers, she gave it a soft push and it swung open farther, revealing a short, narrow hallway with light coming from rooms on either side.

"Hello?" she called. "Mr. Peyton? Are you there? It's Penny Brannigan."

With a glance back at Victoria, who shook her head, she slid into the hallway and inched her way along. She peeked into the first room, a tidy, uncluttered bedroom. She continued down the hall and peered into the second room.

And there, sitting in an easy chair, was Andrew Peyton, who seemed to be asleep. He did not move so she crept quietly into the room, and just as she was about to speak to him, she saw that something was terribly wrong.

He lay back in the chair, his head lolling to one side, mouth and eyes open. He was an ashen grey, and she sensed before she touched one of the cool hands that rested on the armrest that he was dead. Covering her mouth with her hand, she backed away out into the hall and, whispering to Victoria, "I think he's dead," scrabbled in her bag for her mobile. She called the emergency telephone number, gave the address, asked for police and an ambulance, and the two them stood in the hall to wait.

"We should probably wait out here, but we've got a few minutes before the police get here," Penny said. "Do you want to go in and have a look?"

"No, thank you very much!" Victoria shuddered.

Unable to resist, Penny ducked back into the flat and stepped into the bedroom. Careful not to touch anything, she looked at the paintings on the wall and then moved farther down the hall. Nothing looked out of place in the bathroom, and the kitchen was orderly, with the dishes put away. She returned to the sitting room and, without looking at Peyton, took in as much of the room as she could. It was a comfortable, if dated, room and nothing seemed disturbed.

She couldn't tell if anything was missing. She then went back down the main hall and went through the magazines and other mail that had piled up on the table near the door. Nothing was addressed to Peyton.

"Victoria, there's something wrong in that sitting room. Something's not right, but I'm not sure what it is. Go and have a look!"

"Of course, something's not right. You said there's a dead person in there. Are you crazy?"

Penny gave her a gentle nudge.

"Go on. Please. So we can talk about it later. Second door on the left."

"What am I looking for?"

"There's something odd about the room. Something's not right, but I don't know what it is."

Victoria exhaled and groaned, then dashed into the flat. A few moments later she was back, out of breath and shaking.

"Maybe I shouldn't have asked you to do that," Penny said.

"Too right, you shouldn't have!" Victoria moaned, bending over and covering her mouth with her hands. "I think I'm going to throw up! I've got no stomach for this sort of thing. Don't forget, Penny, I was there at the spa when those bones were found. I don't know how many more bodies I can take."

Minutes later a uniformed police officer arrived.

"Down the hall, second door on the left." Penny pointed the way. Seconds later another police officer pounded after him, followed by two paramedics, and then the police officers they had been hoping to see.

"Now, why am I not all that surprised to see you here?" Davies asked, looking from one to the other. "Are you all right?"

Penny nodded. "I'm okay, but Victoria's feeling a bit queasy."

"Bethan here will stay with you and take your statements, if you feel up to giving them now. If not, they can wait. I'll be back as soon as I can."

He continued down the hall and followed the others into the flat.

"Would you be okay if I left you for a moment?" Bethan asked. "I just want to pop in for a moment and see for myself."

Penny nodded.

"It's not you I'm thinking about," Bethan said. "Victoria here is looking decidedly peaky."

"Too many bodies," Penny said. "The bones at the spa and now this."

"Hang in there and I'll be back in a minute. Maybe you could just sit down here, Victoria, and I'll be back as soon as I can."

Victoria slid down the wall and sat on the floor under the stairs, back against the wall, legs out in front of her, and her head in her hands.

Penny crouched down and put her hand on her friend's

shoulder. "I'm really sorry," she said. "I shouldn't have asked you to go in there. That was really stupid of me."

Victoria groaned. "Help me up and let's get out of here. What are we waiting for, anyway?"

"Bethan wants to take our statements, but I'll just tell her that we need to leave. She'll understand. They know where to find us and we can do it later. Be right back."

But just as she was about to re-enter the apartment, Bethan emerged and Penny asked her if they could leave.

"I don't think Victoria's okay to drive," Bethan said, frowning.

"We didn't drive. We came on the bus."

"Oh, really. Wait there." She ducked back into the flat, and moments later, wearing a reassuring smile, she was back, standing beside Victoria.

"The boss says I'm to drive you two ladies home. Won't take long and I'll take your statements when I get there, if you're up to it."

They drove in silence back to Llanelen, Victoria in the front seat, leaning against the headrest, Penny gazing out the window at the green fields that bordered the rural road.

"I'll come in for a cup of tea, if that's all right with you," Bethan said as they reached Penny's cottage. "I'll put the kettle on and you two sit. You've had a shock."

Penny and Victoria sat down in the sitting room, facing each other. The atmosphere was tense and heavy.

"I don't know what you expected me to see," Victoria said in a low voice, with a glance toward the kitchen where Bethan was putting on the kettle.

"I'll talk to Bethan when she comes in," Penny said. "I can't tell you how sorry I am."

Bethan joined them in a few minutes later with a tea tray and poured out cups for each of them.

"When you looked at the body, Bethan, did you notice anything strange?" Penny asked. "There was something odd there, but I can't put my finger on it."

"He looked very calm to me," Bethan replied. "There was no sign of anything amiss, and the paramedics seem to think he died of a heart attack. Probably natural causes. He was fairly elderly, after all."

"Maybe."

Bethan took their statements and then left.

"I'm starting to feel a bit better," Victoria said. "I could probably eat something, if you're buying. Or cooking."

Penny smiled. "Of course. Giving you a nice meal is the least I can do. Do you know, in all that, we didn't get the coloured nail polish for Eirlys. I'll have to go back to Llandudno soon to get it for her."

"Well, you're going on your own next time."

"And what about tonight? You won't feel up to a meeting with the gang. I think I'd better ring them and tell them not to come. And next Friday is that opening in Liverpool that we wanted to go to, so I'll tell them to come in a fortnight and we'll bring everyone up to date. We should have lots more information by then.

"Fancy a pizza, since I'm on the phone, anyway?"

. . .

The next week went by uneventfully. Work continued on the spa, lost time was made up, and Eiryls and Penny sat side by side in the salon, polishing and painting. She rang Davies from time to time, but there was no real news. Because Andrew Peyton had died suddenly, an autopsy was conducted, but it revealed no cause of death. Perhaps when the toxicology reports come back, Davies had suggested. The bones found in the ductwork remained unidentified, although acting on Penny's hunch, Davies had asked Merseyside to try to locate dental records for a Cynthia Browning. But dentists retire or sell their practices and X-ray records are lost or destroyed. The human bones were thought to be at least thirty years old, and the smaller skeleton found with them was determined to be that of a small dog. Both skeletons were female but bore no marks of obvious trauma.

Seventeen

I've really been looking forward to this," Penny said to Victoria on the train to Liverpool the next Friday. "It feels good to get away. It's been a long week." She leaned back in her seat, glanced at Victoria, who was sitting in the seat opposite her with a magazine in her lap, and then looked out the window. She watched a few scattered buildings go by, and then shifted her attention to Victoria. Scanning a fashion magazine, her ghostly reflection in the window, she was occasionally turning a page with a small sigh, whether of envy, boredom, or exasperation, Penny could not tell. When she turned the last page, she dropped the magazine onto the empty seat beside her, put her glasses on top of her head, and leaned back and closed her eyes, her hands resting lightly in her lap.

Penny continued to gaze at her but was not seeing her. She

was seeing the body of Andrew Peyton in his sitting room, dead in his chair. And what was now striking to Penny was the sterility of the scene. There were no reading glasses on his head as if he'd just dozed off, no book or magazine in his lap, no television or radio playing. Nothing. Is that the way people are when they're alone, she asked herself. No! They do something, especially with their hands. They're on the computer, or knitting, or holding a book. They're watching TV and the remote control is in their hand. That's what they do when they're alone. So what had Andrew Peyton been doing before he died? He had probably been with someone. Talking, perhaps.

Victoria's eyelids fluttered and she opened her eyes. When she saw Penny, she gave a little start.

"It's all right," Penny reassured her. "We're on the train to Liverpool. How do you feel?"

"Have you ever fallen asleep on a train?" Victoria asked.

Penny nodded.

"Well, that's what I feel like. Like I need a cup of coffee."

"That's a good idea. We should be arriving at the station soon, and we can get a coffee before we go to the gallery."

"While you were dozing, I think I figured out what was wrong with the scene when we found Peyton," said Penny when they were seated with their coffee in the Lime Street station.

Victoria shuddered. "Hmm, there's something not quite right here," she said, with an exaggerated hint of sarcasm. "Oh, now I get it, there was a dead body in that chair."

Penny gave her a sharp glance.

"I know you're still a little sensitive on that subject," she said smoothly, "so I'll overlook that." She then went on to explain her theory that Peyton had been talking to someone when he died.

"And that would explain why the door was open; someone had just left. The police didn't seem too interested in that. Gareth said they are not treating Peyton's death as suspicious, but I think it is."

She looked at Victoria over the rim of her cup.

"And there's something else that bothers me. They couldn't find a cause of death. The paramedics thought he'd had a heart attack, but it turns out from the autopsy there was nothing wrong with his heart. Oh, a bit of clogged arteries, as you'd expect to find in someone his age, but not enough to cause a heart attack."

She looked at the paper cup.

"God, I hate these paper cups. Make the coffee taste like blech!" She blew a light raspberry. "Do you know, when I first moved to Britain, train stations had cozy little restaurants where you could get a glass of wine or a pretty bad cup of coffee. But at least they were served up in proper glasses or cups and saucers."

Victoria nodded. "Yes, I remember those days. God, we sound absolutely ancient when we talk like that. Anyway, do you think Peyton's death is somehow connected to what happened to Alys?"

"I think it has to be. I think she was murdered for her art. Her brother, the vet, told Thomas and Bronwyn that their mother was surprised that she'd left so little work behind. But she had a show coming up, so the work must have been there. The thing is, what happened to it? There are only the two pieces we know about . . . Emma had one, and Jones the lawyer had the other."

She took a sip of her coffee.

"I haven't been able to find any local dealers who ever handled an Alys Jones painting, and because her work isn't on the market, she isn't known. She should have been known or would have been, if she'd lived. She was a very talented painter, you know. So to answer your question, I think Peyton knew something. Either about Alys's death or the art."

Victoria nodded. "Or both. And let's assume the bones are Cynthia Browning. Do we think whoever killed Alys killed her, too?" Victoria asked.

"We do," Penny replied. "And about the same time, too. It may be that Cynthia overheard something or asked one question too many. And Alys's killer or killers decided she had to be silenced."

"That was really awful about the little dog, though," Victoria said.

Penny nodded and winced. "Very nasty."

She drained the last of the coffee from the paper cup, snapped the plastic lid on it, and then peered into Victoria's empty cup.

"Well, ready to go?"

They walked sedately up Brownlow Hill until they reached the gothic building that not only anchors a University of Liverpool neighbourhood but gave its name to the redbrick university movement of the late 1800s. They stood for a moment, heads back, to admire the famous Liverpool landmark with its spires, turrets, and gracefully arched windows.

As the bells in the clock tower tolled the hour, they passed through the entranceway and found themselves in a magnificent great hall, now used as a modern café. Faced with gleaming brown and blue terra-cotta tiles, the walls and archways were stunning. The columns, covered in shell-shaped brown tiles, were especially impressive for their smooth regularity. Admiring the interior as they went, they climbed the shallow stairs to the first floor.

With smiles and nods, they accepted glasses of wine from a young man holding a tray standing outside the adjoining rooms where the exhibit had been mounted.

"Real wineglasses, not that plastic rubbish!" Victoria grinned as she tipped her glass in Penny's direction. They eased their way into the room and joined the small crowd. The exhibit was a multimedia retrospective of artists from the 1960s and included a large display case filled with drawings and sketches by Stuart Sutcliffe.

"He was a friend of John Lennon and . . ." Penny stopped when she realized Victoria wasn't beside her. She looked around and saw her gazing at a painting on the far wall. The evening light pouring in through the tall, graceful window slanted down on her, touching her blond hair with little beads of sunshine. Victoria turned slowly, seeking out Penny with her eyes, then pointed at the painting.

Penny joined her and gasped.

"Don't you think this looks a lot like yours?" Victoria said softly.

211

The painting showed a woman sitting in a striped deck chair, reading, with a brick wall behind her. She held a book in one hand and gently brushed the hair from her forehead with the other. She was wearing a summery white frock lightly sprinkled with delicate purple splashes.

"Mine?" asked Penny. "My painting or my garden?"

She leaned forward to look at the signature on the lower right of the painting and then said the name out loud.

"Millicent Mayhew."

"If Millicent Mayhew painted that, I'll eat my hat," said a voice from behind her.

Penny turned around slowly to see an elderly woman planted squarely behind her. She was wearing a burgundy plaid skirt with matching jacket and a fussy blouse with frothy lace spilling down the front, struggling to break free of the lapels. The woman pointed at the painting.

"Mediocre Milly we called her. She could no more have painted that than I'm an Olympic ski jumper!"

"Who do you think did paint it, then?" asked Penny.

"I've probably said more than I should have," the woman replied. "It's just my opinion, that's all." She started to turn away, but Penny put a hand gently on her arm. "Please, I'd like to talk to you." She gave Victoria an imploring look and gestured in her direction. "My friend Victoria here and I are looking into the hit-and-run death of an artist about thirty-five years ago, and we think there's a connection to this woman."

The woman's face softened and a subtle light came into her blue eyes.

"Do you mean Alys Jones?" Penny nodded eagerly. "She was a lively one, so full of fun. Really brightened the place up."

212

"You knew her then?"

"Oh, yes," said the woman. "I knew all of them. Alys and Cynthia, and Millicent and her creature. That awful man. Oh, what was his name?" She tapped the side of her head.

"Andrew Peyton?"

"That's it. He was a nasty piece of work, but he had nothing on Millicent. She had a special genius for making people afraid of her."

Penny's eyes darted quickly around the room. Important-looking men in dark suits were chatting up twenty-something long-haired girls in jeans and skimpy tops. Nothing new there, she thought.

"Look, I'm sorry, let's introduce ourselves. I'm Penny Brannigan and this is Victoria Hopkirk. It's a long story, but we'd love to talk to you. Maybe this isn't the best place. Somewhere quieter. Would you join us for dinner?" The woman hesitated, and Penny realized that from her age and dated suit, she was probably a pensioner on a very mean budget. She had likely come to the opening thinking the free wine and whatever food was being served would do for her supper, and that would be one less meal she had to worry about. "Of course, it would be our treat," she added. "Do let us give you a nice dinner. Anywhere you like."

"Well, I haven't been to the Adelphi in many years, so that would be rather nice," the woman said. "If you wouldn't mind. I don't know what it's like there now, of course."

"I'm sure it will be just fine," Penny said. "Would you like to go now, or shall we walk around for a bit and look at more of the exhibit?"

"Well, we could have a look at it on our way out," the

213

woman said. "I've seen them all before. I was surprised to be invited, to be honest. I only came to see if there was anybody here from the old days, but there aren't many of us left. All died. Or been killed off."

She gave Penny a sharp, knowing look.

"Why are you here?"

"We came hoping to meet you. Or someone like you. We just didn't know who you would be." Penny paused. "Who are you, by the way?"

"Oh, didn't I say? My name is Florence Semble. I was the secretary at the School of Art for many years, and I knew all of them. And yes, before you ask, I knew Lennon. And a jumped-up little git he was, too. So aggressive and rebellious. Still the music worked out all right for him, I'll give him that." Her eyes clouded over as fifty years slipped away and an image of the disruptive eighteen-year-old Teddy Boy with the drainpipe trousers, duck's arse haircut, and affected working-class accent filled her mind.

Penny smiled and turned back to contemplate the Mayhew painting, while Victoria and Florence moved on.

Half an hour later, as they left the gallery, Victoria turned to Florence and asked if she would be all right to walk to the hotel or if she would prefer that they hail a cab.

"I walked up the hill," she replied tartly, "so I can certainly walk down it!"

About twenty minutes later, Penny pushed on the revolving door of the Adelphi and they all entered the grand old hotel.

Built in 1914 to cater to upper-class passengers of the large liners whose home port was Liverpool, the Adelphi still manages to evoke the gracious era of oceangoing travel.

As they crossed the reception area, Florence turned to Penny and Victoria and gestured up the red carpeted stairs.

"Oh, I haven't been in here in years," she said. "It's grand to be back. We should just see if we can pop into the Sefton Suite up here. It's an exact replica of the smoking lounge aboard the *Titanic* and well worth seeing."

She led the way through the *Titanic*-sized ballroom and up a few side stairs to a doorway and peeked in. "There, girls, have a look at that!" She waved Penny and Victoria into the room, where they stood, eyes turned upward.

From the massive chandeliers hanging from the soaring ceiling, to the ornately carved oak-paneled walls, the oval-shaped room, which represented the full-blown luxury of the Edwardian age, was spectacular. As they drank in the beauty of the room, a disembodied voice startled them.

"Sorry, ladies, we're just going to start setting up for an event, so I'm going to have to ask you to leave."

Reluctantly, they returned to the reception area and then went down the few stairs to Cromptons Restaurant.

When they were seated, Penny explained that she had inherited Emma's cottage and wanted to know everything she could about Alys.

"She was a lovely girl, was Alys," said Florence. "Just a tiny little thing, but so talented. She was younger than the teachers they usually hired at the college, so she had a good rapport with the students. They all adored her. Everyone was so shocked when she died like that. No one could quite believe it. We didn't want to believe it."

"Can you tell me more about her circle of friends?" Penny asked. "The people she hung out with?"

"Well, there was Cynthia Powell. No, sorry, that was another Cynthia. Cynthia Browning. Not sure what happened to her. I think there was talk around that time that she was emigrating to Australia or New Zealand, although I don't know why she'd want to do that."

Florence gave Penny a quizzical look. "From the sounds of you, you're from away, though, so I guess you'd know why some people decide to leave a perfectly nice country and go and live in another one."

The waiter handed them menus, and conversation stopped while they studied them. Florence scanned hers greedily and opted for a smoked salmon starter with roast lamb for her entrée. When the waiter had taken their orders, she continued.

"Anyway, then there was that Andrew Peyton who was on the fringe of it. Didn't really belong to the college but liked to be around the artists, as if some of their creativity might rub off on him."

She took a sip of wine.

"I could never figure him out, to be honest. He was a very queer duck. And I don't necessarily mean queer in that way. Or maybe I do. We could never figure out if he leaned to the lavender. There was something asexual about him, to be honest." She shrugged. "It's anybody's guess what team he played on. Or if he played at all, really. But he was devoted to that Millicent for some reason. Maybe she had some kind of hold over him. Couldn't stand her myself, but maybe that's just me. She was aggressive in a very sneaky kind of way, and although she was somehow unsure of herself, I think she usually got what she wanted."

"What do mean, exactly?" Victoria asked.

216

"She was so fearful that somebody else might have something she didn't, or do something she couldn't. Catty, smiling to your face and saying the most awful things about you behind your back. I never trusted her. Something about her just didn't sit right with me. I like people who are straight up. Me, I speak as I find, and if that hurts people's tender feelings sometimes, then I'm very sorry, but at least with me you'll always know where you stand. That Millicent would put a knife in your back and wouldn't give it a second thought, if she thought it would get her what she wanted."

Florence gave a little sniff and then glanced longingly in the direction of a waiter.

"She never bothered to pretend in front of folks she considered the lower classes, though. She thought we were all common. That was the word she used. As if she wasn't the commonest one of the lot."

"Florence, you said at the gallery that you don't think Millicent painted that work on display—" Penny began.

"What I actually said was that if she did paint it, I would eat my hat," Florence interrupted.

Penny smiled. "Yes, you did say that. But I'm wondering, if not Millicent, then who?"

Florence gave her a wry, withering look.

"Missy, you already know who painted it, and that's why we're here having this lovely meal."

Florence sighed. "I tried to tell all this to the Liverpool police at the time, but they took no notice of me. Why should they? I was just a young secretary. What did I know? They were skeptical when I told them I didn't think it was an accident. They told me it wasn't their investigation, that they'd pass on what I told them to the police who were looking into it, but I never heard from anybody." A cloud of profound sadness drifted across her face. "Oh! Wait! I'm wrong. I did hear from someone. I spoke to Alys's mother. She came to the college one day asking about the paintings that Alys left behind. Millicent was in a classroom at the time—she taught lettering, by the way—and I told Mrs. Jones that Alys never painted at the school but always in her little studio on Rodney Street and that Alys was keeping her paintings well under wraps. She didn't want anyone to see them until the big show that was coming up in the spring, I think it was. Or maybe it was late winter, I can't remember. Her mother said that she and Alys's father had been to the flat to clear out her things, but there were no paintings. So she thought the paintings must have been at the school. But they weren't."

She shrugged. "But they had to be somewhere. I think they were stolen."

Penny nodded. "We think they were stolen, too. But I haven't been able to find anything by Alys Jones in circulation. We know where two are in Llanelen, and there's maybe this one at the Victoria Gallery that we saw today, so where are the rest of them?"

"We didn't see anything in Peyton's flat," said Victoria.

"Oh, him. Yes, I read about his death in the newspaper," Florence said flatly. "Can't say I'm particularly sorry."

"We think he was murdered," Penny said.

"Do you really?" Florence's eyes lit up and she leaned forward. "Now that is interesting. Why do you suppose someone would go to all that trouble after all these years?"

"After all these years?"

218

"Well, yes. I would have thought that if someone were going to murder him, it would have been done ages ago. Could have saved the rest of us all those years of suffering through his loathsomeness."

Penny and Victoria had to laugh.

"You don't like the two of them very much, do you?" Penny asked.

"No, I don't," Florence said, slapping her hand gently on the table. "And don't you find that we instinctively know whether to like or dislike someone? And that our instincts are usually right?"

She nodded at both women and then looked at her watch.

"I'm sorry, girls, but I'm getting a bit tired."

"Just one last question," Penny said. "I think"—she glanced at Victoria, who gave an encouraging nod—"that is, we think Millicent Mayhew had something to do with the death of Alys Jones. What do you think?"

"I think what I've always thought," said Florence grimly. "I think they both murdered her. I think she drove him to it."

The three women sat in silence, surrounded by the usual restaurant din of conversation and clattering dishes. A waiter walked by balancing a large tray filled with sweets, and two women in smart dresses swished past their table on their way to powder their noses.

"You've been so helpful," Penny said finally as they finished their coffee. "Here's my contact information, and I wonder if I could have yours. We may need to speak to you again."

Florence wrote out her information and handed Penny the slip of paper.

"Here you go," she said. "It's in the Waterloo area. Do you know it?"

"No, I'm afraid I don't," Penny said, "but I'd like to give you the money for a taxi home."

Florence protested weakly, and then took the £20 note.

"I'll just see myself out," she said, "and thank you for the evening."

Victoria and Penny followed a few minutes later and saw her hurrying down the street in the direction of the buses in Queen's Square.

"Come on," Victoria said. "If we hurry, we can catch the eight-twenty train. Lots to talk about on the way home. We'll have to decide what to do next."

"What we have to do next is go to Llandudno and meet Millicent. I hadn't thought that they both were in on it. I thought it would be one or the other, but it makes sense."

"Does it?"

"Yes, because that explains why she killed Peyton. Because he was the accomplice. As Florence said, 'He was her creature.' I think he had decided to tell what he knew, and she killed him to silence him."

They waited for the light to change and then started to cross the street.

"We just have to figure out how she did it."

Eighteen

With autumn closing in, the velvety greens of summer that cloaked the timeless hills were giving way to the reds and golds of early fall. Thorny bushes bursting with plump, ripe blackberries lined the hedgerows, and the fields were dotted with grazing sheep, their fleeces thick and heavy against the coming winter. It had been almost two months since Penny had been sketching and she missed it. In the company of an artist friend or two, she enjoyed the leisurely Saturday morning or Sunday afternoon rambles along the pathways, across the fields, and up into the high hills with their panoramic views of the towns and villages spread out below.

By lunchtime, the fine mist that had shrouded the town as folks made their way to morning church services had dissipated, and the afternoon promised to be clear but cool.

Dressed warmly in anoraks and sturdy boots, and carrying their painting gear, Penny and Alwynne strolled alongside the Conwy River and then cut across the fields toward Gwydyr Forest, on the eastern edge of Snowdonia National Park. Alywnne had chosen their destination, saying to Penny she had a hunch the spot she had in mind would intrigue and interest her.

The way was steep for the first couple of kilometers, as the path led them away from the valley and up into the shadowy glades of the forest. Finally, they arrived at a small clearing where they set down their wooden painting cases and shrugged off their backpacks. Alywnne produced a flask, and they sat on their small painting stools, wrapping their hands around warm mugs of tea and lifting their faces to the sun.

"Would you like to set up here?" Alwynne asked, "or carry on to the lake? I'd prefer the lake, but we have to keep an eye on the time. It gets dark so early now, we should aim to be back in town by six."

"The lake, I think," said Penny. "The view here is wonderful, but the lake isn't much farther, and in this light I expect it will have a lovely shimmer to it. I'm sure it'll be worth it."

They packed up their tea things and carried on climbing.

"You know," puffed Alwynne, "I do envy those ramblers who just have to worry about themselves. They don't have to do this climb carrying all the gear we've got."

"That's true," agreed Penny, "but we have something interesting to do when we get where we're going. They just eat lunch."

They continued along the path, which had been laid down

a century ago by miners working the nearby, long-abandoned lead and zinc mines. They headed deeper into the forest until they caught their first glimpse of Llyn Parc, a long narrow lake surrounded by thickly wooded slopes leading down to the water's edge. They found themselves in a sheltered glen and watched for a moment as a kestrel circled slowly overhead, casting a long, sweeping shadow.

Penny put down her painting case, folded her arms, and looked about.

"I'm not sure if I've been here before," she said. "It looks vaguely familiar, but I know I'd remember that trek and I don't. And I don't think I've ever painted here."

"But someone you know has been here," said Alwynne, pointing across the glen.

Penny followed the sightline of her finger and gasped.

In front of her was a stand of what looked liked tall, dying weeds, but she realized that in early summer it would be a mass of brightly blooming wildflowers.

"They were here!" Penny exclaimed. "This is it! This is the spot where the picnic paintings were done. Emma and Alys were here."

She looked around more carefully. "Of course, it's much more overgrown, but I know this is it! I can feel it."

She headed toward the edge of the clearing, set down her stool, and started removing painting items from her case. Out came a portable easel, a sketchpad, and pencils.

"I'm going to set up here."

"I'll set up right beside you," said Alwynne, "but I'm going to face the other way and paint the lake."

They were soon deeply engrossed in their work, the sound

of their pencils and brushes occasionally drowned out by birds calling to one another across the treetops.

"Penny," Alwynne said hesitantly.

"Hmm?"

"Something's been bothering me."

Penny stopped sketching, her pencil poised in mid-air, and looked at her friend. "What is it, Alwynne?"

"Well, it's like this. If Emma and Alys were, you know, what you said they were, it surprises me that you haven't found any photographs of them together. Or at least you'd think Emma would have had photos of Alys. It seems to me rather strange that you've given the cottage a pretty good going-over and haven't turned up any photographs. Doesn't that seem odd to you? Don't most people keep photos of the person they love?"

Thinking of the one photo she had found in the Harrods pencil case, the young blond woman with the fox terrier pup, Penny nodded in agreement.

After about an hour, Alwynne stood up and rubbed her hands together. "My fingers are starting to get a bit numb with the cold," she said, reaching into her pockets to see if by any chance she'd left a pair of gloves in there last winter. "We're going to have to pack up soon and start heading back to town, I'm afraid."

Penny nodded vaguely and continued sketching, raising her head now and then to look at the scene in front of her.

"So I'm going to take lots of photos of the site for both of us so we can carry on with these at home," Alwynne said.

Penny nodded again, and Alwynne strolled around the clearing, snapping photos of the site from all angles for Penny and the view of the lake for herself. She replaced the camera in her backpack and began gathering up her sketching materials.

With a sigh, Penny began to do the same.

"You're right," she said reluctantly, looking at the sky and then back to the tall grasses in front of her. The sun had shifted toward the west, taking with it the light that had given the scene intense colours just an hour earlier. Long shadows began to creep in all around them. "We're losing the light."

The women finished, packed up their gear, and as they prepared to leave, stood for a moment looking around them. Alywnne touched Penny's arm. "You're thinking of them, as they were that day."

Penny felt the salty sting of unshed tears and nodded.

"I can almost feel them here." She gave Alwynne a fleeting glance and then shifted her shoulders to position her backpack more comfortably.

"I've been thinking that if we'd known then what we know now, it might have been nice if they'd been cremated and their ashes scattered together here."

Alwynne pursed her lips. "You might be right," she said gently.

They set off for home the way they had come and eventually reached the clearing where they had had a cup of tea on the way up.

"There's a bit more tea left," said Alwynne, "if you'd like to stop and rest for a few minutes. I've got a couple of Welsh cakes here, too."

"You have the tea," Penny said. "I've got a bottle of water, but I'd love a cake."

Alwynne unwrapped the small, flat, raisin-studded cakes and offered one to Penny.

"Mmm, this is delicious," Penny said. "Where I come from, we'd almost call this a pancake, but it's sweeter. This one isn't store-bought, is it?"

Alwynne shook her head and laughed.

"My husband makes them. He was looking for a hobby when he retired, and I thought he'd take up gardening or lawn bowling or rambling, like any other man would do, but he chose baking. It all started, really, when he was clearing out his mother's house and found his grandmother's old bake stone. Couldn't bear to part with it. So he cleaned it up and started using it. Says it brings back memories of his grandmother's baking when he was a boy."

"Hmm," mumbled Penny with her mouth full, waving a hand and shaking her head to decline Alwynne's offer of a second cake. She swallowed and then commented, "I imagine his pastime doesn't do your waistline any good, but other than that, it seems harmless enough."

"Oh Penny, it's easy to see you're not married. If you were, you'd know that the downside is that it doesn't get him out of the house!"

She wrapped up the remaining cake, tucked it into her backpack, and they continued on their way.

As they approached the scattered buildings that signaled the town was about to come into view, Alwynne returned to the topic she had raised earlier.

"I think you need to keep looking for those photos, Penny. I'm sure Emma would have had pictures of Alys that were taken while they were together, and she would have kept them stashed away somewhere. They'll turn up, you'll see. You'll find them."

They trudged on and soon reached the town square. Alwynne was planning to drop off her painting gear at the town museum where she worked and meet her husband in the pub. The two women stopped for a moment to say good-bye, and then Penny continued the last leg of the journey home on her own.

As she turned off to walk the last few hundred metres down the lane that led to the cottage, she heard a vehicle coming up behind her. The sound grew louder, and as she turned her head, an SUV approached. As it came nearer, she realized that it was not slowing down and she moved quickly to the side of the road. She was almost on the grass verge when the speeding car brushed by her. Just as she dropped her painting case and dove into the rowan bushes that lined the narrow lane, she caught a fleeting glimpse of two lads in the car, laughing and shouting over loud rap music. And mixed in with the music was the sound of a barking dog. The meet was over in a moment and the vehicle disappeared.

Penny landed on her side and instantly felt a sharp stab of pain shoot through her right shoulder. Holding her arm, she struggled to sit up and then shakily raised herself until she was standing. She stumbled out of the undergrowth and back onto the lane.

"Oh, no," she groaned. The wooden painting case that she had taken everywhere with her since her student days lay in splinters all over the roadway, smashed tubes of paint leaking Winsor & Newton colours everywhere. She picked up what she could carry and then, because her cottage was only a few more metres farther, decided to go home, phone Gareth, and return to the scene with a bag to pick up the tubes of paint before it got dark.

"No, I'm okay," she said when she reached him on the phone. "My shoulder hurts a little where I landed on it, but I'll be fine. No, I don't want to go to casualty. I'm going back to get the paints and what's left of the case, and then I'm going to have a bath."

Gareth suggested that she should not be alone and that he could be there in about an hour, and she gratefully agreed and rang off.

After grabbing a plastic bag from a drawer in the kitchen, she returned to the lane, and as the sun started to slip behind the tall trees that ranged in the distance, she hurried toward the remains of her painting case. Making sure the roadway was clear, she bent down in the middle of the lane and scooped up the pieces of the case and its contents. She returned to the cottage and, after locking the door behind her, went upstairs for a bath.

The pain in her shoulder had become constant and throbbing, and she hoped the warmth of the bath would soothe it. Soaking seemed to help, and half an hour later, wearing clean jeans and a chunky sweater, she came downstairs, closed the drapes, turned on the lights, and then looked around in the fridge to see if there was anything she could offer Gareth for dinner. Scrambled eggs, maybe, if he wasn't too fussy.

A few minutes later he knocked on the front door, and, smiling, she let him in. He put his arms gently around her and held her.

"You poor thing! I'm glad you're okay," he said as he released her, "but you're bound to be a little shaken up. Come and tell me all about it. I'm afraid I'm going to be in policeman mode. Did you get a good look at them? What about a license plate number?"

They sat on the sofa, facing each other. Penny tucked one leg under her.

"It all happened so fast," she said. "All I saw were two lads, but I doubt I could describe them. It was a silver-coloured SUV. Land Rover, I think. Couldn't see the license plate number, but I heard very loud rap music. Oh, and they had a dog with them. It was barking really loudly. Almost frantically, now that I think about it."

Gareth leaned toward her.

"A barking dog, eh? We've just had a report from a farmer out Pen-y-Pass way saying his prize Border collie's gone missing. Well, this helps. At least we know what kind of car we could be looking for. Excuse me, I'll just phone that in."

Penny stood up and, wincing, reached for the bag of painting materials she had collected from the laneway. She waited until Davies was finished with his call and then held the bag open so he could see inside it.

"Look at the mess they made of my case. And not only that," she said, pulling a few pages of sketching paper from the bag, "they ruined my afternoon's work. It took Alwynne and me hours to hike to that clearing and back, and I spent a couple of hours on those sketches. And wait until you see what those nasty little beggers did to it!"

She turned the sketch over, with a smile, and there, in all

the red, blue, yellow, green, and black glory of Winsor & Newton paints, was a clear tire imprint.

Davies laughed.

"I hope you'll let me buy you a new case and set of paints. The boys at the lab are going to love this."

Nineteen

O n Monday, Penny made the familiar journey to Llandudno, and this time she stopped at the beauty supply
depot to pick up the candy-coloured nail polishes Eirlys wanted
so badly. The yellows, turquoises, and bubble-gum pinks made
Penny cringe, but if that's what her young customers wanted,
who was she to disagree? She didn't mind about something as
trivial as nail polish colours, but on the matter of the tanning
bed she was holding firm. No tanning.

Holding an inexpensive bouquet of carnations under her
arm, she climbed the stairs of the Sunset Villas Retirement
and Nursing Home. The door was locked, but a receptionist
looked up when she saw Penny and pressed the buzzer that unlocked the door.

Penny smiled her thanks as she entered the reception area.

It was meant to be tastefully and reassuringly decorated in timeless floral prints, but the area looked outdated and horribly overdone. Farther down the hall that stretched in front of her she could see elderly people, some walking about aimlessly with empty, vacant looks, holding onto the rail that ran along the walls, others dozing in parked wheelchairs. Trying to assume a briskness that would convey she knew where she was going and what she was doing, she headed off in the direction of the seniors.

"Excuse me!" the receptionist demanded. "Who are you here to see?"

Penny shifted the flowers under her arm, turned around, and approached the desk.

"I'm here to see Millicent Mayhew." She hoped she looked a little more confident than she felt.

"Just a minute while I check. Are you on today's visitors list?"

"No, I'm not. I didn't know I had to get on a list. I thought that as I was in the neighbourhood, I could just drop in."

The receptionist softened. "Yes, of course you can. It's just that if we know in advance, we can put you on our list. We like to know who's coming and going. I expect you'll find Miss Mayhew in the dayroom. First door on your right. Please sign in here and then go on through."

"Thank you."

Penny did as she was asked, then retraced her steps and headed back along the corridor. You never forget the smell of a nursing home, she thought. When she had first arrived in Llanelen all those years ago, she had earned a bit of extra money giving manicures to the ladies in the seniors' home.

Word spread, and the manicures became so popular that she was soon able to open her own business. She wondered if anyone ever came here to do manicures and made a mental note to suggest the idea to Victoria.

Admitting that her heart wasn't really into weekday sleuthing because she felt anxious if she was too far away from the building site, Victoria had decided to stay behind in Llanelen. There were contractors to oversee, materials to monitor, invoices to prepare, and all the rest of it. She had also reminded Penny that they now had two businesses to run—one in development and one that needed to be generating income.

It wasn't fair to dump all the work on Eirlys's young shoulders, she said, adding that she hoped Penny would get her investigation wrapped up soon so she could focus on her work.

"I didn't sign up for this, you know," Victoria had warned her. Penny had apologized and promised to get down to business right away. Or at least on Tuesday, at the latest.

She entered the dayroom and hesitated. She had no idea what Millicent Mayhew looked like.

"You look lost, young lady," said a man in a wheelchair near the door. "Who are you looking for?"

"Millicent Mayhew."

"Oh God, what do you want with that old cow? I know you're not a relative because you've never been here before, and you're not a friend because she hasn't got any. So what do you want with her?"

He stiffened slightly. "Not a cop, are you?" Then he answered his own question. "No, you don't have the look of the police about you."

Penny thought for a moment. She had been tempted to tell

him that the reason for her visit was none of his business, but remembering the endless boredom and isolation that many seniors in nursing homes experience, she quickly reeled that thought back and decided to humour him. And something about his cheeky smile and earnestness appealed to her.

"Know a lot about the police, then, do you?"

"Used to."

Penny nodded, grinned, and pointed to an empty chair across the room in front of large windows that overlooked a well-kept garden.

"Could we sit over there and have a little chat? Would you like a push?"

She walked across the room pushing the wheelchair and then parked it so her new friend was turned slightly toward her but was still facing the room. Then she sat down, placed the carnations across her lap, and turned to him.

"I'm Penny Brannigan. I live in Llanelen. It's a very long story, but I think Millicent might know something about a hit-and-run accident that happened a very long time ago. I want to talk to her about it. You seem to know her. Would you tell me about her?"

"Nice to meet you, Penny. I'm Jimmy." He held out a cool, dry hand for her to shake. She could almost feel the bones inside it, but his grip was strong and firm.

"Actually," said Penny, "I don't even know what she looks like. Is she here?"

The two surveyed the room. Elderly people, some wearing bibs, sat in chairs or wheelchairs, most gazing vacantly into space. A wall-mounted television set was tuned to an all-news channel, but no one took any notice. Personal-care aides in pastel-coloured uniforms flitted about hauling someone up straight in a chair here and patting a shoulder there. Occasionally someone shouted out, startling the others.

"Depressing, isn't it?" asked Jimmy. "And don't think it won't happen to you. So enjoy the time you've got left before it does."

"How long have you been here?"

"Almost two years, for my sins. My legs don't work as well as they used to, but the rest of me, including the important bits, works just fine, in case you'd like to know."

Penny laughed. "Too much information, thanks just the same, Jimmy."

He placed his hands on his knees and gave her a sly look, then gestured with his head across the room.

"That's her over there by the television. In the pink blouse."

Penny followed his gaze. Millicent Mayhew sat slightly to one side of the television, looking out the window, showing her profile.

She had a large pile of false grey curls on top of her head, with upswept hair beneath them. As Penny watched, Millicent raised a hand and patted the back of her head, gently pushing the hair upward. She turned her head slowly and, seeing Penny, narrowed her eyes and gave her a belligerent scowl. Penny felt a shiver run down her spine. If you were having a nightmare about Joan Crawford, she thought, this would be the look of pure evil that would leave you paralyzed with fear.

Penny turned back to Jimmy. "I see what you mean. Tell me about her."

He cleared his throat. "Nobody likes her. Nobody trusts her. She cheats at cards. They only let her play bridge with them because she's good at it, and there aren't that many bridge players around who still have it up here." He tapped his temple. "If you know what I mean." Penny nodded.

"She keeps to herself. Doesn't allow anyone in her room. What's she got in there that's so valuable? Even I've never been inside her room, and a locked door never stopped me before."

Penny raised her eyebrows.

"Yeah, back in the day I did a little breaking and entering, among other things."

"Oh, so that's how you know the police."

"It's how the police know me, more like."

He leaned closer to Penny. "I don't think you'll get very far talking to her. She won't care what you think or what you suspect. Why should she?" He tapped Penny on the arm. "I think your time would be better spent having a look around that precious room of hers."

He nodded. "She lives on the ground floor, just down the hall. Why don't we take a look-see?"

"What if she goes back to her room?"

"They're going to set up for a game of cards in a minute. That'll keep her out of the way. Tell you what. I'll wait outside the door, and if I see her coming, I'll give you the signal and we'll bugger off out of there."

Penny straightened up in her chair and nodded at him.

"I think you're right. Let's go."

"Not so fast. This requires a bit of planning. You're forgetting a few things."

"What?"

He held up a hand and mouthed *gloves*.

"Right!" Penny whispered.

"Wait here." Jimmy scooted off in his chair and returned a few minutes later with a small blanket over his legs.

"Ready? Let's go. You push."

The two left the room, aware of many pairs of curious eyes following them.

They proceeded down the hall at a leisurely pace, until Jimmy told her to stop. The door to the room was open.

"I thought you said—"

"This isn't her room," Jimmy interrupted. "Hers is two doors down. Here you go," he said, reaching under the blanket on his lap and pulling out a pair of purple latex gloves. "Put these on. And this," he added, handing her a white jacket. "Obviously you don't watch enough films, or you'd know when you're up to something or when you're in a place where you've got no business being, you should try to blend in. People who look as if they belong can go just about anywhere. Now give me your credit card so I can get the door open. I like American Express, if you've got one. They've got a bit more give in 'em. Gets the job done faster."

Penny handed over a Visa card.

"Sorry, this is all I've got."

"Well, it'll have to do, then, won't it? Right now, girl, push me up to her door and then stand beside me so you're on the side facing toward the dayroom." Penny did as she was told. Jimmy fiddled about for a few seconds, listening intently, smiled, and then gently pushed the door open.

"In you go. I'll wait here. And another thing. You always need to plan your escape. If I start to sing 'It's a Long Way to Tipperary,' you need to get out right away, pull the door shut behind you, and push me off to the right. There's a lift there,

237

and we can hide out on the second floor until the coast is clear." He gestured with his head. "Go!"

Penny slid through the door. The room was dark, with curtains drawn. She switched on the light, turned slowly around, and then gasped.

The room was an Aladdin's cave of paintings. Almost every inch on every wall was covered with artwork. Reeling from the impact they made on her, Penny peered at one and saw the signature she was expecting, in the lower left corner. "A. Jones." And another and another. "A. Jones." "A. Jones." Views of Liverpool and Llanelen, all done in the distinct Alys Jones style that Penny had come to recognize. She couldn't take them all in. She walked slowly around the room, trying to count them but feeling so frightened she had to stop at twelve.

Grateful for the gloves, she yanked open the top drawer of the bureau and riffled through the contents. Nothing. She moved through the other drawers and saw nothing unusual. By now her heart was racing so fast she thought she would collapse. And just as she pulled open the drawer on the bedside table, she heard Jimmy starting to hum softly.

She felt an unbearable tension, trumped by an irresistible drive to continue. She flipped over the contents and felt her fingers wrapping around a small vial. There were two, and a syringe. She glanced at the label. Potassium chloride.

She shut the drawer, closed the door behind her, grabbed the handles of the wheelchair, spun Jimmy around, and headed down the hall.

"Please be there," she said, trying to catch her breath. The lift was there and they clattered on, pushed the button for the second floor, and a few moments later, found themselves in a small sitting area. Penny bent over, with her hands on her thighs to catch her breath, then threw herself into a chair and placed her hand over her heart.

"Did you see what you wanted to?" Jimmy asked.

"Oh, yes, and then some," she said with a gasp. "Just let me catch my breath."

Jimmy watched as she slowly recovered the ability to speak.

"By the way," she asked, "did you ever meet a Detective Inspector Davies?"

"I remember a Sergeant Davies. You didn't want to get on the bad side of him, but he treated you fair, like."

"Well, good," said Penny, reaching into her handbag for her mobile. "I'm glad you liked him because you're going to be meeting up with him again in a few minutes."

"Aw, now, wait a minute, Penny," said Jimmy. "Steady on. I was just trying to help, that's all. And now you're calling the cops on me."

Penny looked aghast.

"God no, Jimmy! Not you! Milllicent. Gareth's going to be very grateful to you when I tell him what you did."

"Oh, Gareth, is it now?"

Penny nodded as she spoke a few words into her phone.

"He'll be here in a few minutes."

"Well, in that case, here's your credit card back."

He looked a little sheepish.

"And your bank card. Oh, and the twenty pounds I owe you."

Penny laughed.

"Jimmy, you're incorrigible! I've had my purse with me the whole time. How did you do that?"

He cracked his knuckles and grinned at her.

"Kind of exhilarating, isn't it?"

Twenty

$\mathcal{P}$enny looked at the list of clients in the appointment book. "Thursday already! Another week almost gone. Mrs. Lloyd was right when she said it would be Christmas before we know it."

Eirlys peered over Penny's shoulder as she set her coffee down.

"Mrs. Lloyd's coming in this morning, see," Eirlys said, pointing to an entry. "And she's bringing her friend with her. They're both to have a manicure, then they're going shopping, and tomorrow they're going to Manchester for the weekend. She told me all about it when she rang up for her appointment."

Penny nodded and smiled at her.

"And Mrs. Lloyd said she hoped you would not mind too

much, but she would like to have her manicure with me to-day."

"Eirlys, where would we be without you?"

She glanced at her watch.

"Our first client won't be here for another fifteen minutes, so I'm going to leave you in charge while I nip up to the library. I've been meaning to photocopy something, so you keep an eye on things here, and I'll be right back."

Eirlys looked dismayed.

"But what about your coffee? I made it just the way you like it."

Penny took a small sip.

"It's delicious, Eirlys, and it is just the way I like it, but a wee bit too hot. By the time I get back, it'll be just right. Just leave it in the back so it doesn't get spilled on the appointment book. Won't be long."

She snatched up her purse and bolted out the door while Eirlys browsed the selection of nail varnishes, looking for one or two that would appeal to the salon's most discerning client.

Mrs. Lloyd made her grand entrance right on time, accompanied by a small, pleasant-looking but nondescript woman of similar age.

"Now, Bunny, let me introduce you to the girls," said Mrs. Lloyd. "Penny, Eirlys, this is my friend, Bunny. Well, I say Bunny—her name's really Mavis, but we've always called her Bunny." Penny showed Bunny where to sit, and the filing and soaking of the manicure ritual were soon under way.

The two clients chatted with each other about their weekend plans for a few minutes, and then Mrs. Lloyd looked across at Penny.

"Now, Penny, we've known each other a long time, and I know you've been looking into the accident of Alys Jones. I must say, I was rather surprised you haven't consulted me yet, but never mind. I have done something on your behalf. I had a word with Morwyn." She turned to look at Bunny. "You remember Morwyn, Bunny, my niece who works for the newspaper. She went through the archives or whatever you call it, old newspapers and she found an item that relates to this. She made a copy for you," she told Penny.

Mrs. Lloyd pulled her wet hand out of the soaking bowl and looked at it.

"Oh."

She smiled at Eirlys.

"Eirlys, love, just fetch my handbag, would you, dear?"

When Eirlys returned with the bag, Mrs. Lloyd asked her to open it, remove a folded piece of paper, and give it to Penny.

"I think you should read it later, Penny, not now. Read it when you get home tonight. And now, Bunny here has something she wants to tell you. You'll remember I told you that she used to drive the post office van. She was on her round that morning and she saw something."

Feeling the pit of her stomach clench, Penny raised her eyes from Bunny's hand to her face. The tension in the room rose, and Eirlys, picking up on it and clearly uncomfortable, released Mrs. Lloyd's hand and wiped it with a towel.

"Should I step out for a minute, Penny?"

Penny looked at Mrs. Lloyd, who nodded.

"I hadn't thought of that, but we don't want to upset you, Eirlys, love. Tell you what. Why don't you take a couple of pounds out of my purse and go and get us some nice biscuits, and when you get back, we'll have a nice cup of tea?"

"What kind of biscuits would you like, Mrs. Lloyd?"

"Whatever kind you'd like. Something with a bit of chocolate on them, perhaps?"

Eirlys jumped up out of her chair and, clutching the money, left on her errand.

"All right, Bunny," said Mrs. Lloyd, sitting back in her chair and folding her arms. "Get on with it. Tell Penny what you saw that morning."

Bunny nervously cleared her throat.

"It was very early," she began, "just before dawn, and I was making my rounds, dropping off the mail to the sub–post offices and clearing the pillar boxes as I went. It was crisp and cold, I remember, and I thought it was going to be a lovely day.

"And while I was in Trefriw to empty the letterbox there"—she looked at Mrs. Lloyd for reassurance—"you know the one, Evelyn, just outside the pub." Penny and Mrs. Lloyd both nodded. "A car stopped and asked me for directions. It seemed odd to me that someone would be out and about at that time of day looking for the back route to Llanelen."

Penny thought for a moment and then rose from her seat and went to her handbag. She returned with the photocopy she had made at the library that morning and, pushing the soaking bowl aside, put it down on the table, facing her client.

"Have a look at this photocopy of an old newspaper clipping," she said. "I know it's not very clear, but do you recognize this man? Was he the one driving the car?"

Bunny stared at the image of four people, one holding up a piece of art and the other three pretending to judge it, and she then shook her head.

"No," she said, again shaking her head slowly, "he wasn't driving. In fact, he wasn't in the car. I don't know anything about him."

Penny sighed.

"But this one," Bunny said, "this one was in the car and she's the one who asked me for directions." She pointed at Millicent Mayhew.

Penny covered her mouth with her hand and looked at Bunny.

"So she did it," she said softly.

"But she was the passenger," Bunny continued. Her damp finger hovered over Millicent's image and then moved on. "This girl," she said, pointing to the smiling blond woman, "this is the one who was driving."

Her finger came to rest on Cynthia Browning.

Stunned, Penny struggled to take it in.

"But why didn't you come forward and tell all this to the police at the time, Bunny?"

"Well, they were all over the radio asking for information, but they always referred to the driver as 'he,' so I figured they were looking for a man. I reckoned the police knew what they were talking about and they knew who they were looking for and it was a man. I didn't see any man that day, just these two women." She shrugged. "Still, I always wondered about it. Something didn't seem quite right."

Penny and Mrs. Lloyd exchanged a quick glance, and then Penny nodded slowly.

She remembered Gareth's comment a few days earlier when he looked at the tire tracks across the painting—how the boys in the lab would enjoy it. She was certain that women worked in the lab, too. It seemed that policemen still talked like that.

"I see now what it was. It was the times. Back in 1970, the police—mostly men, of course—would just assume the driver was a man, and they would use 'he' in their appeal for help."

She thought for a moment.

"But this happened such a long time ago, Bunny, and you did that route every day. Why do these two women stand out? How is it, do you think, that you even remember them?"

"I've thought about that day a lot over the years, Penny. When I heard about what happened to that poor young woman and realized I was so close to the scene, I wondered about it. It just stayed with me. And also, it was my daughter's second birthday that day, and I was in a hurry because I wanted to get through my rounds early, if I could, so I could pick up a few bits and pieces for her party."

"Oh, and Gwennie, I wondered if you could make us some of your delicious sandwiches? There'll be about ten of us, including a couple of pensioners from out of town, so we want to make it a bit special. And those little petit fours you do so beautifully. Lovely! I'll leave the rest up to you. Thanks and we'll see you tomorrow."

Penny put the phone down and turned to Victoria.

"There. All set. We're giving a nice little tea party tomorrow to thank everyone. That was a really nice idea of yours to invite Florence and Jimmy. They probably don't get out much, and I'm sure they'll really enjoy it. Gareth and Bethan are bringing Jimmy with them from Llandudno. Jimmy says he hasn't had a ride in the back of a police car for ages, so it'll be quite like old times!"

Victoria remained silent.

"You've been absolutely wonderful about all this, Victoria, and I promise you've got my full attention now. We'll get the spa ready for a Christmas opening, and they're starting work on the cottage next week so it's going to be all go. No more mysteries, I promise."

"I don't mind the mysteries," Victoria said, "but you've got to get your priorities straight." Penny was looking so intently at the photo of Alys as a child that Victoria gave up. "And blah, blah, blah."

"You're absolutely right," Penny agreed. "And I will. Now let's go over the guest list one more time. Oh, I forgot Mrs. Lloyd. She's meant to be going to Manchester tomorrow, but I'll invite her anyway and she can decide whether she wants to come."

Penny added her name to the list.

When Victoria left, Penny settled into the sofa with her handbag on her lap and withdrew the piece of paper Mrs. Lloyd had given her earlier. After setting the handbag to one side, she unfolded the paper. It was a clipping from the local paper, dated January 21, 1971.

She scanned the article, noting that the coroner had returned an open verdict, and the police were continuing their efforts to find the driver responsible.

Then, a few paragraphs into the story, the words of the coroner caught her full attention.

This driver failed completely to observe the ordinary decency one expects from a motorist involved in an accident—to pull up and go back to help the injured person," said Coroner Morgan Llewellen.

"I hope the person who is responsible for this fatality can be brought to justice in another court."

The coroner said that in the circumstances he would only ask the jury to return a verdict concerning the medical evidence that death was from shock due to multiple fractures of the pelvis and that the cause was being struck by a motor vehicle. The jury agreed.

She sat there for a few moments, then rose, crossed the room, and pinned the paper to her whiteboard.

Twenty-one

On Friday afternoon, the guests arrived, crowding eagerly into Penny's sitting room. Gwennie passed around sandwiches and Victoria and Penny handed out cups of tea and glasses of sherry for anyone who wanted one.

"And the important bits work just fine," Jimmy was overheard telling Florence as she not-so-discreetly wrapped up a few sandwiches and slipped them into her handbag.

Mrs. Lloyd, with Bunny in tow, had arrived amidst a great air of business and bustle, and then the two of them monopolized Florence as they reminisced about the old days, when young people showed respect to their elders and you could get a decent cup of tea and a nice homemade bun at a wonderful tea shop filled with atmosphere, not like those American chains of coffee shops where surly girls with hair in their eyes serve overpriced, bitter coffee with pretentious names.

And then Davies stood up and asked for everyone's attention. A silence fraught with delicious anticipation filled the room.

"I'd like to begin," Davies began, "by thanking Penny and Victoria for hosting us this afternoon and by thanking you for coming. Each of you here today has played a role in helping us solve a crime committed many years ago."

He glanced at Alys's two brothers.

"And the lives of two of you were changed forever because of what happened on that December morning so long ago.

"Penny has asked me to tell you what happened, so I'm going to do that for you now."

Mrs. Lloyd breathed deeply and leaned forward.

"Alys Jones was killed in a hit-and-run accident because, as Penny came to suspect, Millicent Mayhew was filled with an all-consuming envy. She couldn't accept that Alys was on the brink of great recognition as a superbly talented artist. She wanted that fame for herself, so she killed Alys and then stole her artwork.

"Her original plan was to take the paintings, cover up Alys's signature, and then sign them herself. She did this with one painting—the one on view at the Victoria Gallery that Florence here recognized as not being Millicent's work."

Florence nodded.

"Millicent also realized, too late, that the art world would never accept the work as hers—too many questions would be asked—so she just kept them, lived with them, and loved them. They were well worth having in their own right so in that regard she was a bit like a private collector who will pay a fortune for a stolen work of art, knowing that it can never be exhibited. It's a private pleasure kind of thing.

"Originally, we thought that Peyton was driving the car that hit Alys, with Millicent in the passenger seat. In fact, it was she who pulled the body off the car and left it on the side of the road."

He looked at the Jones brothers and apologized softly.

"Now, as for our second body, the remains found in the ductwork of the new spa. I have just been on the phone with Cynthia Browning's brother, who was rather tired after a long flight from New Zealand. Browning had been out there to a family wedding at which Cynthia, now a great-grandmother, had enjoyed herself enormously."

A ripple of chatter passed through the group.

"Then who . . . ?"

Davies pinched his lips together.

"That's the thing. We don't know whose remains they are. We think they might be a homeless person or transient who disappeared and was placed in the ductwork at some time when the building was either a hostel or was being used as a squat. So we'll keep looking into that."

He gave his audience a few minutes to take in this new information.

"So, with Cynthia alive and well, we will start extradition proceedings to bring her back to the U.K. We aren't sure yet what her motive was, but hopefully we'll be able to discover that when we speak to her."

Florence cleared her throat and held up her hand.

"Excuse me, sir," she said, "but I might be able to help with that."

251

Davies smiled at her. "Yes, go on, please."

"Well, Cynthia had set her cap on this young man from New Zealand. He came from a wealthy family of sheep farmers, with large holdings, apparently. They got engaged, but while he was back in New Zealand, she had a brief fling with someone else and found herself in the family way."

A few brief smiles flitted across elderly faces at the use of this quaint, old-fashioned euphemism for "pregnant."

"Anyway, she was so afraid he'd find out—and you have to remember that back then, abortions were illegal and very risky. But Millicent knew someone who could help, because her brother's girlfriend had been through the same thing. So she got Cynthia sorted out, and I think Cynthia then owed her. Big time."

Florence paused and looked around the room.

"Millicent was like that. She'd get something on you and then hold it over you." She thought for a moment.

"Oh, all this takes me back. They set me up with a little desk in the corner of the staff room because there was no place else for me, so I had to try to get my work done in there while the teachers went on and on about their personal lives. And you should have heard them talk about how much they disliked the students! Makes you wonder what they were doing there if the kids were that bad. It's the old adage, I guess, 'He who can does . . .'

"Anyway, they talked about anything and everything and took no notice of me. It was as if I didn't exist. So I just kept my head down and got on with my work. But I overheard a lot, I can tell you."

Davies glanced at Bethan, who nodded.

"Thank you, Florence," he said. "We'll get Sergeant Morgan to take your statement later. You've been very helpful."

Florence sat back in her seat and folded her arms.

Penny stood up. "Sorry to interrupt, Gareth," she said, "but before we move on, there's something I'd like Florence to see."

She crossed over to the small desk, picked up the Harrods pencil case, and pried it open.

"Is this Cynthia?" she asked Florence, showing her the black-and-white photo of the smiling blond woman cradling the fox terrier.

Florence took the photo from Penny, tipped it toward a nearby lamp, and gazed at it. Then, she turned it over.

She nodded slowly.

"Yes, it is. Cynthia's parents had a home on Menlove Avenue. She lived there with them, and they took in students." She looked around the room.

"You have to remember that Liverpool was badly bombed in the war, and even twenty years later there was still a housing shortage, so many Liverpudlians, who had the room, took in student lodgers for a bit of extra income."

She handed the photo back to Penny, and all eyes turned back to Davies. But before he could speak, another voice spoke.

"Florence is right."

Jimmy looked at Florence and smiled.

"Millicent is still like that. I think she finds out things about the staff members and uses that information to her advantage. She always gets special treatment, and I think it's because they're afraid of her."

Florence patted his hand, and they turned their attention to Davies.

"And now, we come to our second victim, Andrew Peyton," Davies continued. "He was given a massive injection of potassium chloride by, of course, Millicent Mayhew. She might have overheard two nurses discussing it. It's the perfect poison, really. It's in your body anyway; your heart needs it to function properly. But an overdose will stop the heart. And it's easily available in a nursing home. It's on every drug cart, and it's not restricted in any way.

"It was our old friend Jimmy here who remembered all the commotion a couple of weeks ago when Millicent couldn't be found for the bridge game and how annoyed the players were when they had to rustle up a fourth at the last minute."

Jimmy nodded and looked very pleased with himself.

"We've also found a witness who saw Millicent entering Peyton's building that day." He paused and looked around. "I'll be happy to answer any of your questions later, but right now, Alys's brother, Richard, would like to say a few words."

A respectful silence settled over the group as Alys's twin rose to his feet. He handed his teacup to his brother and turned to face the gathering.

"I want to thank all of you for your efforts. Alwynne, who found the photos, the rector who spoke to my brother, and Penny and Victoria who tracked down the people who killed our sister."

He paused for a moment to fight back tears.

"You know, when someone is murdered, everyone tends to focus on the victim. But there are more victims. Our mother was bewildered and in pain for the rest of her life, our father was consumed by hatred for her killer, and our whole family ached with the loss of our beautiful girl. Her death changed who we were as individuals, and it changed who we were as a family.

"And then there was Emma. She lost the love of her life, and because of the attitudes when all this happened, she felt she couldn't discuss it with anyone or come forward with what she might have known. She had to carry a terrible burden for the rest of her life. If our family had only known, we would have tried to comfort her.

"And we can't even begin to imagine what the art world lost. We're glad that her paintings are being restored to us. The value hasn't been determined yet, but we understand they're valuable. Of course, we'd be only too happy to exchange all of them for her."

His voice broke, and unable to continue, he returned to his place. Bronwyn immediately went to him and said a few words. He smiled at her and conversation resumed.

And then the rector took the floor.

"I have been asked to speak to a somewhat delicate matter. When Alys died, her family did not know about Emma, but now that they do, her brothers have asked for her ashes to be reburied in Emma's grave. They feel that the two belong together, and we are making the arrangements for this to happen. We'll let you know when."

Gwennie, who had been listening at the entrance to the sitting room, entered the room and passed among the guests with a tray of sweets.

Penny gave her a grateful smile as she went through to the kitchen, where she picked up a large parcel wrapped in brown

255

paper. She returned with it to the sitting room where Richard Jones was preparing to leave.

"Richard, I'm very sorry. I know I should have returned your painting sooner, but here it is," Penny said, as she handed it to him. "I've put the other one in there, too. Like Emma and Alys, they belong together and I want you to have both of them."

Richard smiled at her and then at his brother, Alun.

"Funny you should be thinking that," Richard said. "We thought the same thing, and hoped you'd be willing to swap. Anyway, we thought you'd rather have another one."

Alun returned and handed Penny a painting. She turned it around, and a broad smile lit up her face. It was the painting of Emma reading in the garden.

"I love it," she said, "and a restorer will soon get the signatures right. Alys's signature will be here, under this gob of paint. A gob of paint very badly applied, I must say."

The brothers thanked her again, shook her hand, and then made a dignified, graceful exit.

The party gradually broke up, with Florence and Mrs. Lloyd among the last to leave.

"You may not have seen the last of me," Florence said to Victoria as they were saying good-bye. "Mrs. Lloyd here has offered to rent me a room, and I might take her up on it. I could live so much more cheaply here, and there's nothing much keeping me in Liverpool now."

"And the company would be very nice," added Mrs. Lloyd as they made their way together down the path leading to the street. "I have a feeling we're going to get on just fine. In fact, why don't you stop over tonight? I've got a nice fresh chicken we could have for our supper. Do you like to cook, Florence?"

•   •   •

That night, as Penny lay in bed thinking over the events of the day, she smiled as she thought of Mrs. Lloyd and Florence. Both so opinionated. What was it Mrs. Lloyd had said about Emma? "Always liked to have the last word." Now, that was the pot calling the kettle black!

She started to drift off to sleep and then jerked awake.

The last word! Of course!

She flew down the stairs and into the living room. She pulled the Scrabble game off the shelf where Gareth had placed it on her first morning in the cottage and carried it to the table. She ripped off the elastics holding the box together and lifted the lid. Her shoulders sagged with disappointment when she didn't see what she was looking for, but she couldn't resist picking up the little pad on which Emma had recorded the games. She flipped to the last page. With a score of 278, Emma had won, and even noted a word which she must have liked for some reason: QUEENLY!!

Penny lifted out the folded board and the four tile racks and set them on the table. Then she picked up the little bag containing the letter tiles, kneaded it for a moment, and then opened it and tipped out its contents. The letters of the alphabet scattered across the table, and so did dozens of photographs. She picked one up and tipped it toward the light. Alys and Emma with their arms around each other in front of the Victoria Gallery & Museum. Emma smiling and waving to the camera. Alys lounging in a deck chair, holding a glass of wine. And so many more, capturing all the golden moments of their lives together. Penny's heart began to beat faster as she lifted out the

257

cardboard inserts that divided up the space. And there they were. Four slim red journals. She looked at the years: 1967, 1968, 1969, 1970. Peeking out of the 1970 volume was an envelope. She withdrew it from the diary and turned it over. It was addressed to her.

She opened it, and began to read.

My darling Penny,
By the time you find this, you probably know my secret.
You'll find all the details in the journals, but I want you to
know that I loved you, too, in a different way. You reminded
me of her and when I met you . . .

I'd better put the kettle on, thought Penny. It's going to be a long night.